I0784020

CARLY SPADE

One

Boom. Bada boom. Bada boom. The repeating bass from the blaring music reverberating off the walls in the club had become static noise to me as of late. It used to give me life, making me want to double fist with a wine bottle in one hand and a whiskey in the other, partying until the sun rose. Not that I could see myself doing anything else in the Cove, but its grandeur had started to lose its luster within the past year. And I blamed a temptress with crimson *hair*.

"Boss," Tambie yelled, her black pixie haircut bobbing as she stomped her foot when I hadn't answered her on the second beckoning.

I'd crawled into my favorite spot in the establishment—a corner rounded booth with burgundy crushed velvet upholstery and large enough to seat ten averagely sized beings. With my arms sprawled on the back, I tapped a finger to the music's steady rhythm and lazily turned my gaze on her. "Yes?"

Tambie rested the silver tray she'd been carrying on the grey and white marbled table between us, flattening her palms on either side of it. "I know you prefer your *you* time—" She shifted her gaze to the side and mumbled, "—a lot lately." Her eyes didn't turn back to me until after she nervously scratched the tip of one of her small, tan, fawn antlers extending from above her temple.

The sight made the spot on my skull itch where my own much larger horns made an appearance when I allowed them, but I resisted the urge to touch my head there. "Has the club lost business? Caught on fire? Has a stampede of centaurs suddenly burst through the doors, destroying everything in their path?"

Her brown eyes blinked, and she flicked the collar of her black button-down uniform shirt. "No?"

"Then it seems that my lack of involvement hasn't affected business. So, my dear little maenad, what's the problem?"

Tambie clucked her tongue against the inside of her cheek and folded her arms in a huff. "Sir, when people come to *Bacchus*, they expect its owner to be on *theme*."

Arching a brow at her and ignoring her eyes rolling as I turned in my seat to survey my establishment, I continued to drum my fingers to the music. Violet and white light spilled in rotating rays across the main dance area on the first floor; dozens of gyrating bodies swayed and bounced to the rhythm. Several more female maenads danced between Corinthian columns bordering the top floor while male demons of varying colors patterned between them, their spade tails twirling to the music.

Whichever patrons weren't dancing were either taking up stools at the bar or chatting away at one of the many lounge areas or tables. Club Bacchus turned no one away, and it was apparent from this night alone with its variety in attendance— gods, witches, minotaur, demons, gargoyles, sprites, griffins, and even a leprechaun or two. And this was a *slow* night.

With a deep sigh, I turned my gaze back to Tambie. "Seems like everyone is doing just fine without my company."

Tambie leaned her forearms on the table and curled her finger in the air, beckoning me to pay attention. "Listen, Dion. They *talk*."

"They?" Propping my elbows on the table, I rested my chin on my palms and grinned. "Sounds scandalous. I'm *almost* intrigued."

After Tambie let out a lion's cub growl, she swiped the tray and shrugged. "Fine. It's your club, D. All I do is schlep drinks, right?"

Regret twisted in my gut, but by the time I swallowed my pride enough to open my godsdamned mouth, Tambie was already sulking away, her steps rivaling a minotaur's hooves.

"Tambie," I called out. "I didn't mean it like that." Sighing at Tambie ignoring me with her back firmly turned, I rose from my seat to try again, "Tambie."

She proceeded to act as if I were invisible and busied herself with taking drink orders. Grumbling, I slumped into my chair and checked my phone—still no new messages. It'd been *months* since I'd heard from her. A growl bubbled in the back of my throat, and I slammed the device to the table, screen down. A sudden chill washed over my skin, causing my spine to stiffen. It only took one quick whiff to recognize *that* scent.

Tossing a glare at the entrance, my grip tightening on the lounge chair, I ground my molars. "A primordial. The icing on the fucking cake today." After snapping the collar of my dress jacket and ruffling my hair, I pushed to standing, working my way toward the entrance to reluctantly greet our VIP guest.

It wasn't easy to discern which of the primordial gods he was through the seas of dancing bodies. But as I got closer, smiling and nodding to those who addressed me, the primordial slid into a squared lounge area in the corner, and our eyes locked.

Erebus. As if it could get any fucking worse.

"Emo," I announced, playing with the golden grape charm hanging from the chain around my neck. "To *what* do I owe this displeasure?"

Erebus peeled off a pair of black leather driving gloves, for whatever the fuck reason he needed those, and tossed them to the table before bothering to look at me. "Dion. I had a feeling this establishment was yours."

Flagging the bartender, I silently ordered drinks delivered to the table and took a seat without invitation. "And *what* gave it away?"

"What brought you to Arcane Cove? Weren't you gallivanting with the likes of mortals for years across North America?" Erebus flicked some of his long black hair from his equally dark eyes and motioned for his lackeys to give us space.

"I was."

Aella, another maenad, approached with drinks, resting them on the table with a wicked glint in her eyes as she devoured Erebus with her stare. The chestnut ringlets of her hair bounced when she pressed the empty tray to her chest. "Can I get you anything else?" She directed the question at Erebus.

"No," Erebus quipped, not giving her more than a quick glance at her antlers.

Aella's demeanor turned instantly, and I delicately snatched her wrist, knowing she was seconds away from giving the primordial a warranted piece of her mind. "Thanks, Aella."

Another of my maenads stormed off, slamming her heels offbeat with the music. At least this time, it wasn't my fault.

"I was in North America for a time, yes," I continued, sliding one glass to Erebus and raising mine. "But I got tired of hiding my true nature. What can I say?"

"Oh?" Erebus flicked his gaze to my hornless forehead. "Did someone saw them off?"

Godsdammit. Why did it have to be a *primordial* who waltzed into my club?

"Tartarus, no." Leaning my elbows on the table, I lifted the glass between us, flashing a sinister grin. "Why? You miss 'em?"

"*Yámas*, you prick," Erebus said deadpan and clinked his glass against mine.

Guzzling half of it down, I wiped my sleeve across my mouth. "And what about you? Aren't you supposed to be in Chicago?"

"I got *bored*." Erebus eyed the alcohol suspiciously after taking a swig. "Is there ambrosia wine in this?"

Smiling proudly, I interlaced my hands behind my head and leaned back. "And that's why my place is the most popular spot in town. Because only at Bacchus can a mythical, paranormal, or fairytale creature find a buzz."

"Fitting," Erebus scoffed, resting the glass on the table. "I decided to move the business away from humans."

A black bear sauntered past us, following a woodland nymph toward the bar. The bear shifted into a hulking male clad in leather pants before curling an arm around the nymph's waist and sitting on a stool.

"And you chose to bring it to a place with some of the most dangerous beings in the universe? Gee, Bus. The Cove is a *great* place to run an organized crime outfit."

A rare smirk bordering on a subdued smile quirked Erebus's

lip. "Precisely. What's it to you? You're not the Cove's sheriff, too, are you?"

"No. That's Herb. A porcupine shifter." Shaking my head, I leaned toward the primordial and lowered my voice. "I don't give a rat's ass what you do with your time, and considering the gods and primordials have an agreement, I don't have a choice but to look the other way." Erebus's glass had gone empty, and I pressed a finger to it, magically re-filling it. "But you bring that shit into my club, and I'll have a little chat with my pops about releasing the Titans again out of *spite*. Do we have an *understanding?*"

Erebus's jaw clenched, his ominous gaze casting shadows between us. After giving a curt and barely noticeable nod, he pointed at my bare chest beneath my jacket. "It seems you've forgotten how to get dressed."

"What?" Pretending I hadn't realized I wasn't wearing a shirt, I peeled open my jacket and snapped my fingers. "Nope. I'm positive my shirt is right where I left it—" I paused and downed the rest of my drink, locking eyes with the embodiment of darkness sitting across from me. "—your mom's bedroom floor."

Erebus's hand coiled into a fist atop the table, a smoky halo forming around his head and shoulders.

"But that's right." Interlacing my fingers and resting them in front of me, I let the snarkiest of grins curve my lips. "You don't have one."

"How does it feel to be such an insignificant god that they charge you with sex, frenzy, and festivity?" Erebus arched a dark brow, the shadows billowing around him settling.

Scoffing, I pushed my back to the seat. "Did you just hear yourself?"

"Yes, but these are things most gods delight themselves in regularly between a more meaningful existence." Erebus swirled his hand through some of the inky tendrils near his mouth, producing a cigar. A lackey was quick to trip over the table to light it.

It'd been a while since someone tried to crawl under my skin.

"I don't think you spend enough time around mortals. Sex and festivity are rather high on their enjoyment lists." I raised my hand from the table to above my head and chuckled.

After taking several puffs from his cigar and wasting one more minute of my damn time, Erebus replied, "Enjoyment. Not necessity. Not aspects that enrich or embody their livelihoods."

"I'm pretty sure sex is necessary for human life to continue, or did you miss that day at tyrannical primordial school as a kid?"

Erebus spent ash directly onto the table despite an ashtray resting inches from him, inciting a growl to bubble in my throat. "Fertility. That, when you want to get technical, is necessary. Correct me if I'm wrong, but that jurisdiction belongs to a goddess who tried to have you killed once, right?"

It was old news that my dad and his former queen had an arrangement to take lovers outside of their marriage. My mother was one of his first conquests, and the hatred the queen bore from her pregnancy announcement never bothered me. It was the fact that *my* mother died as a result of it. Fury and frenzy coiled up my spine, firing at the base of my skull.

A vibration went off several times from my front pocket, immediately pulling me from the inferno that'd been building in my chest.

"You're lucky my ass is vibrating," I said to Erebus, pointing a stern finger at him as I stood and walked away, relishing that quizzically shocked look on his dumb face.

Slipping my phone from my jeans pocket, I halted when I saw the notification blazing on the home screen—a text from "Red." The woman I hadn't heard from in months with the fiery auburn hair and my polar opposite whom I couldn't get off my fucking *mind*.

Holding my breath, actually pinching my lips together, I swiped the screen. A random drunken demon smelling of sulfur and tequila hugged my shoulders from the side. As politely as I could, I shoved him away, an equally drunk warlock catching him with a hoot of laughter.

The air escaped my lungs when I read the text message:

Red

Hi.

One word. Two fucking letters. And it was enough to send my ethereal heartbeat into overdrive. She texted me. That meant she was *thinking* about me.

"Tambie, I'm checking the mail," I shouted toward the bar.

Tambie scrunched her nose at me. "You know they deliver it straight to your office, right?"

"The *other* mail," I corrected, raising my brows.

Tambie gave me a thumbs up and hoisted her tray filled with drinks to her shoulder.

Arcane Cove was resplendent during the day with its blue skies and perfectly crafted sunsets, but it was damn near enchanting at night. It could be the night owl in me, but nothing compared to the hundreds of stars blanketing the sky and the moon shining so bright it cast intricate shadows. This was a rare sight in the mortal realm from its vast number of artificial lights dampening it. That wasn't the case in the Cove because any light here came from *magic*.

As I strolled down the sidewalk, my thumb hovered over the reply button, at a loss for what to say to her after all this time. I mean, I, too, could've picked up the damn phone and texted her, but I hadn't. She'd seemed so disinterested in being anything but friends, and to be honest, I'd be perfectly fine with it, but her presence? It created an entirely different frenzy inside me. One I had never felt with any other female *or* male.

Fuck it.

Not wishing to stew on it any longer, I quickly typed up my reply and slid the phone back into my pocket. If she wanted to be friends, I'd be the one who was never short on innuendo and oozing with compliments. And if she wished to take things to the next level, I'd show her a *time* she'd never imagined possible.

Two

Chelsea

Unopened boxes surrounded me that I hadn't bothered to unpack yet. Finding work in my new hometown took priority, and so did the essentials I took the time to set up—my desk, chair, laptop, and bed. Everything else could wait because time was most certainly money, and I had zero clients here. Being a public relations specialist wasn't without its perks, as there were always people in need of portraying a particular image. Whether it was a celebrity, a high-profile lawyer, an entire organization, or an athlete—that last thought stung because one of my most prized clients, an ex-MMA fighter, Harmony Makos, was not only a client but my best friend.

Without her on my roster, I saw little reason to stay around Colorado and made the bold move to pick up everything and seek a fresh start. With Harm shacking it up with her new war god husband and porting all around the universe, it only seemed fitting to start over in a new place. Not to mention, the only other person tethering me anywhere was my sister, Elani, and she, too, no longer lived the everyday life now that she'd become a love goddess. Goddesses. Mythology. Things I'd never imagined were real until this past year when I'd been thrust into this new world by the two most important women in my life living out fairytales.

When I researched new towns and vibes to get out of my usual rut and start fresh, I'd settled on the New England area, given its lush trees and picturesque views during autumn and winter. Surprisingly, though, Arcane Cove was the place that I'd accidentally driven through, and I couldn't turn away once I was here. There was something about it that just felt *right*. The moment I drove past the arched wrought iron entrance displaying the town's name surrounded by endless canopies of vibrant green trees, I knew this would be it. Add on reasonable apartment prices and a twenty-four-hour bakery across the street from my building—I was sold.

Sighing, I stared at the dozen opened internet tabs on my laptop screen. I'd slipped into a tank top and pajama shorts, queued up my ABBA playlist, made coffee, and got to work the moment I woke up, but I felt unmotivated for some reason. One of my feet tapped on the floor, while the other rested on my seat chair, my knee pressed to my chest. I was on my third pen, chewing this one too to oblivion, one of several bad habits I developed whenever I attempted to stop smoking.

Jingling got my attention from behind me, and like a Bond villain, I slowly turned in my chair, already knowing the sound's source. Riley, my black and grey ferret, froze with a set of keys dangling from his mouth. When I first adopted him, he learned things quickly and had been so courageous that I named him Riley. Over time, I realized I should've called him Houdini or Robin Hood, the little thief.

"Riley," I cutely chastised and held out my hand. "You know mama will need those later. Were you planning on hiding them from me?"

Riley stood on his hind legs, his tiny black nose twitching. Grabbing a small bag of ferret treats, I jiggled it and waited for him to scurry over before lowering my palm to him. He dropped the keys in my awaiting hand and pressed both paws against my skin as a form of apology. Smiling at him, I lifted my other hand for him to give a high-five and offered a treat after he performed the trick. Satisfied, Riley darted away, lunging into his flexing tunnel toy.

My grin soon faded from the momentary bout of joy Riley brought me. Arcane Cove wasn't without its lack of potential clients, but approaching them as a newbie resident wouldn't be easy. As ironic as it was, given my occupation, the initial socializing to build a client list was always the most challenging for me. I'd pulled up websites for several local musicians, an author, a film company, an airline, and a travel agency. The only one I'd managed to fumble my way through an e-mail to was a music artist who claimed to bring ancient sounds to their work using handmade instruments and unique performances.

Snatching my phone from my desk, I pulled up a text window to Harm.

Me

Hey. I'm dreading starting over. And bored.

A frown pulled at my lips when Harm hadn't started typing back within seconds. That wasn't typical for her, which meant she was mythically busy, and I probably wouldn't hear back from her in days, possibly weeks. Pulling up another text window to my sister, I typed with a bit more fervor.

Me

Hey. What ya doing?

Waiting, I traced my forefinger over my lips and sprung in my chair when I saw the three dots bouncing from my sister typing a reply.

Lani

Up to my ears in winged toddler duty. LOL. How about you?

A warm grin formed on my lips at the sight of the attached photo with the message. Elani's daughter, Hedone, with her bright red hair, chubby cheeks, and the tiniest pair of tan wings splayed proudly. Her face was covered with what looked like strawberry jam, and it smeared across her shirt and dirtied her hands. A male pair of hands with dark hair wrapped around Hedone's little body, keeping her from flying—Elani's love god husband, Eros.

Me

Oh, I was starting to wonder if moving was a good idea.

Elani immediately replied this time.

Lani

Don't you dare, big sis. You NEEDED this.

She was right. I did. It just hadn't felt that way, given I was alone here and completely starting my business from scratch.

Me

You're right. Who's the big sister here, huh?

Lani

☺ **You've got this, Chels. Talk soon. Love you.**

Me

Love you too.

Growling, I turned off the screen and slapped my palms over my face. Riley circled my leg until he reached my lap, curling up on it. Like second nature, I scratched his miniature head and down the length of his back.

"Riley, buddy, you always know when I need you. You're a little smarty, you know that?"

My ferret rolled onto his back, his bigger canines sticking out over his bottom lip and giving the illusion of a smile as I rubbed his belly.

The song *Lay All Your Love on Me* by ABBA played from my speakers, and my entire being froze. It had always been my favorite song of theirs. I'd belted it out from my bedroom as a teen despite my little sister making fun of how tone-deaf I was. This time hearing it however, created a tingly sensation over my skin.

Leaning back in my chair, I swiveled, closed my eyes, and hummed the familiar tune. Humming turned to full-out singing once the chorus hit, and I stood, cradling an unperturbed Riley in the crook of my arm. The more I sang, the more I felt compelled to dance, swaying and sashaying around boxes stacked in my living room.

The tingles turned to static, sizzling up my spine, swirling and bubbling until it struck my chest and head. I halted, my gaze snapping to my phone resting on the desk. No words could explain the sudden desire I'd felt. I hadn't talked to him in months because I knew in my gut we weren't right for each other. He was oil to my water, an inferno to my tempered simmer. And as much as I'd enjoyed our friendship, given who and what he was,

14

I knew it would have only been a matter of time before things escalated. So why was the phone now in my hand? Why was I about to text him? Dionysus—the Greek god of wine and frenzy. We'd met because of Harm and haven't physically seen each other since, but we texted back and forth every day for months on end. The flirtation was obvious, and toward the end, before I'd stopped entirely, I purposely took longer to respond, making those responses simple and aloof.

"Screw it," I said aloud, pulling up a text window for "Dion," my hand shaking.

What could I possibly say after all this time that wouldn't seem absurd?

Uncontrollably, my leg bounced, and I lifted Riley to smother his head and face with butterfly kisses. He closed his eyes, enjoying every second of affection. It instantly calmed my nerves enough to type.

Me

Hi.

Immediately turning off the screen, I tossed the phone to the desk and waited. They wouldn't write poems centered around my eloquent choice of phrase, but it'd get the point across—I'd inexplicably felt the urge to *talk* to him again. And why was that exactly? Because my favorite song, for the first time, gave me some form of non-alcoholic-induced buzz? That, in some warped sense, it had to be a *sign?*

"*Him.* I'm thinking about Dion like he's just some Joe Schmoe off the streets." I pinched the bridge of my nose and slouched. "He's a Greek *sex* god, Riley."

When I opened my eyes, Riley was alert and bouncing his paws on my stomach. He waited for me to look at him before rising on his back legs and waving his paws, jaw chattering as if trying to speak to me.

"You've never done *that* before, Ri-Ri."

Riley blew out a breath, huffed, and went back to curling up in my lap.

A chime went off on my phone, the screen lit up, and I jolted, staring at the device as if it were about to self-destruct. I chewed on my thumbnail long enough for the screen to dim before snatching it. Swiping it open, my heart raced before plummeting.

Dion

Hey.

"Hey?" I yelled, scrolling up and down as if there was more to the text message I'd missed. "Hey?" I shrieked again, annoyance coiling in my stomach. "We haven't spoken for months, and all he can say is *hey*?"

Riley leaped from my lap right before I stood in fury, holding the phone in a death-like grip.

After taking a long, soothing breath, I tapped my forehead and gathered myself.

At least he had the decency to use *one* more letter, unlike you, Chelsea. Pull it together.

Ugh. How had this guy always managed to get to me the way he had? He infuriated me as much as he made my knees wobble with the way he said things—flirty, sexy, and so irritatingly charming.

I'm still not responding. Not right away. I couldn't in good conscience do such a thing.

Turning, I grabbed my keys and bolted for the door. "And now is a perfect time to check out this bakery. I could really use a cupcake or scone or virtually *anything* sugary."

Riley poked his head out from the hidey-hole in his carpet tower, those dark, glossy eyes plainly *judging* me.

"Don't look at me like that," I grumbled, turning the doorknob and pausing as I looked down at my attire. "I should probably put some pants on first."

Riley quirked his head to one side before disappearing into the hole.

After dressing appropriately and running a brush through my hair to make myself look somewhat presentable, given I wore zero make-up, I headed out the door and descended the two flights of stairs to reach ground level. There, sitting snugly across the street in all its confectionary glory, was the Arcane Cove bakery:

Muffin Compares to You.

Three

I bumped my shoulder into the wooden swinging door of the *Speedy Sandal* establishment, the Cove's only ethereal mailing service. When I stepped inside, it was unusually quiet, but then again, I didn't usually stop by after midnight—ever. Admittedly, it was an excuse to get away from the club and re-gather my thoughts. There wasn't much to the place save for a metal front desk and rows upon rows of mail slots. Within the span of my entering, several of the holes flashed blue or purple, and parcels, scrolls, or letters appeared out of thin air.

"Herm," I yelled, scanning the five-by-five space and seeing no sign of him. Slamming my palm on the bell chime near the computer, I hit it three more times for good measure and shouted, "Hermes, you here?"

"I'm out back, Dion," Hermes' voice responded from outside.

Inviting myself behind the desk, I slid the limp screen door aside and stepped to the vast green meadows situated beyond the post office building. Faint sounds of an electric razor emanated from one of several wooden stalls. Hermes sat on a stool, shearing a black sheep in the dark with only a single heat lamp illuminating his work.

"You're doing that *now?*" I asked, leaning on a support beam and crossing my feet at the ankles.

Hermes paused long enough to shake some of the wool free from the sheep and wipe a forearm over his sweaty forehead. "Been a busy day. Needed to get done, and quite frankly, I find it therapeutic." He gave a lopsided grin, those glacially blue eyes glinting. If I had to compare Hermes' appearance to anyone, I'd most certainly compare him to the likes of a younger, more chiseled version of Clint Eastwood, but I would *never* in Tartarus tell him that. As per his norm, he'd stopped shaving, and his chin bore light brown stubble. "What the hell are you doing here this late, anyhow?" After Hermes raised a brow at me, he finished shearing the sheep.

"Thought I'd check to see if I had any replies from my wanted ad?" I hung my thumbs from my belt loops and waited for Hermes to call my bullshit.

Hermes smirked, patted the now bald sheep on the ass to hurry him along, and stood. "Considering you just sent it out yesterday, bro? No. But Apollo showed interest."

"Sunny can eat a bag of dicks," I clipped, shoving off the wooden beam and dragging my hands through my hair in frustration.

"Olympus, Dion," Hermes huffed, a chuckle following. "I know you aren't our brother's biggest fan—"

"*Half*-brother," I corrected, my words surrounded by a snarl.

Hermes raised his palms. "*Half*-brother. But he offered to headline one night with Apollo's Suns. Could be good PR for the club."

Two cows and a bull moseyed passed us, munching on hay and mooing.

"Nah, see, because the bands I invite into Bacchus haven't publicly flaunted their powers and identities in the mortal realm. Musicians that want a place where they can feel unburdened."

The words flew from my tongue before I had a chance to process them. It sounded uncharacteristically empathetic for me.

Hermes slowly narrowed his eyes. "Spill, Dion. What in the Underworld is going on with you?"

"Nothin'." I sneered at him and turned away.

Hermes didn't buy it, kicking up dirt with his boots as he crossed to me. His hand clapped on my shoulder, jostling me. "Come on, Frenzy. Who's your best bud? Who's your best pal?" He dragged out the "a" in pal and gave a deranged grin.

"What's with that face?" I shrugged him off.

"Alright, I'll guess. You're grumpy because of—what's her name? The one with the fiery tendrils and sparkling emerald eyes?" Hermes clasped his hands under his chin and blinked his eyes like a dame from the old mortal cartoons.

Pointing a stern finger in his face, I brought us toe to toe. "I told you that in confidence."

"You told it to me drunk."

"Even *more* confidence."

Hermes shoved me between the shoulder blades. "Let's go. I'm buying a round or two."

"I'd rather be anywhere right now than the club," I all but whined.

"We're not going to the club. We're going to Finneas', and you, my dear wine god—" Hermes lifted my limp hand and shook it. "—are going to make all our drinks buzz-worthy."

"Fine," I grumbled.

Hermes snapped his fingers. "One second. I need to feed the

animals real quick." Using his speed magic, Hermes whisked away, sending my hair skyward before returning within half a second and dusting his hands off. "Shall we?"

Finneas's pub was something straight out of the mortal Middle Ages with its stone flooring, barreled tables, stools, real candles in the hanging metal chandeliers, and wooden tankards or curved horns instead of glass mugs and pints. A massive oak tree grew through the middle of the establishment, sprouting from the top, magic surging through it, making its veins glow a bright green. Varied types of knight and Viking shields adorned the walls, along with more wooden, stone, and metal accents.

We clamored to the circular bar with a raging hearth at its center and occupied two stools. I pressed my forearms to the wood and rubbed my temples. "Do gods get headaches? Is that possible?"

Hermes drummed his fingers on the bar top and flagged the bartender. "Considering we're not impervious to pain, I'd venture to say, yes?"

Groaning, my face falling into my hands, I didn't notice the pixie edging closer to me until her hand was trailing down my thigh. Lazily, I lifted my head and let my gaze fall to my lap. Her glittered nails sparkled from the overhanging candles, and she ventured further up my leg before I gently took her hand and held it still.

"Flora," I crooned, awkwardly holding her pale hand between us.

Her translucent curved wings flapped excitedly, her wider-than-human dewy blue eyes blinking. Flora perked her pointed ears, cheeks blushing pink before she wound a strand of black ringlet hair around her finger. "Hey, Dion. It's been a while."

"That it has, sweetness." I gave her knuckles a chaste kiss before resting her hand on the bar top near her. "And it's going to be longer."

Hermes's stare burned a hole in the side of my head, but I ignored him.

"What do you mean?" Flora frowned, her wings drooping, and the glitter within her apple cheeks dimmed.

"I—" Pausing, I clenched my teeth.

How the Tartarus did I answer this? It's not like Chelsea was *with* me. I wasn't even sure I had a chance—me—the god of sex *not* having a chance with a mortal woman. The thought only irritated me more.

"Look, Flora. It's complicated, but I'm not looking for company tonight, tomorrow, or for the foreseeable future." Pointing behind her at a very interested troll, I coaxed her attention away from me. "Why don't you go talk to him?"

Flora's cheeks reddened when she caught sight of the brooding blue male with arms nearly as thick as his body. "If you're sure?"

"I'm sure. Run along now before you miss out." After seeing her frolic to the troll, I cracked my neck from side to side.

Hermes appeared in my line of vision with a shit-eating grin. "This *is* about the redhead."

"Yeah, alright." I smacked my hand on the table, making our tankards bounce. "Maybe it is. I *don't* understand how I'm so wrapped up with a singular person, Herm. I've *never* been like this."

Actual concern flooded Hermes's face, which made me uneasy, before it melted into a huge smile at the sight of our tankards arriving.

He slid them toward me, waiting, and after I touched them, lacing the drinks with ambrosia wine, we raised them for a toast.

"To figuring out what makes this one so special, Dion," Hermes toasted.

Grumbling, I lifted my mug and thudded it against his. "*Yámas.*"

"In all seriousness, bro, there has to be something about her. Maybe she's an enchantress?" Hermes said this with such confidence it almost made me laugh.

"She's not. She's just a mortal woman who is a public relations specialist and has a stick up her ass that I've been trying to dislodge to no avail for the past several months." Smirking, I swigged back half my drink.

Hermes rubbed his hand over the newly grown hair on his chin. "That's part of it, isn't it? The challenge? The chase?"

My horns itched beneath my skin at his words.

"You know I love a good chase, and I'm a fucking *master* at it. She doesn't want that." I sliced my hand through the air for extra emphasis, finished my tankard, and punched my fingers against the bar, signaling for another.

"Do you know that for certain? Have you asked?" Hermes gave me his full attention but still couldn't help smiling and winking at a female deer shifter ogling him from a corner table.

"Yeah, Herm, I flat out asked her if she wanted to be chased like a breeding animal." I spread my legs wider, snatching the tankard as soon as it hit the bar top, and changed it into ambrosia wine as it guzzled down my throat.

The very idea of letting my inner beast roam free with Chelsea had my cock half-stiffening in my godsdamned jeans.

"I think you're going about this the wrong way. You're used to females falling at your feet without the need to charm them beyond a smile and a crook of your finger." Hermes turned in his stool, facing me now but still giving the femme shifter knowing glances.

"You act as if you have to do much else, asshole," I scoffed, elbowing him in the chest.

Hermes rubbed his sternum, and after punching me in the shoulder, he answered, "True. But any mortal woman I've been with has been purely carnal. If that's all you wanted with this woman, it would've either happened already, or you would've moved on."

I fucking hated him.

Hunching my shoulders, I brooded over the bar top. "What's your point, Hermes?"

"Dionysus, my godly brother—" Hermes stood and patted my shoulders. "—adapt and overcome. Re-evaluate your strategy and be forthcoming with her. She'd probably appreciate it."

My face contorted into an expression I could only imagine resembled someone who'd witnessed the birth of a centaur. Before I had the chance to make a wiseass comment, however, Hermes slapped my back, shoved his hands in his pockets, and sauntered to the lady shifter.

Dragging my hand over my face, I spied the ornate clock hanging on the back wall displaying an alarming almost two in the morning. "Fuck. I need to close the club. Hermes, do you—"

Hermes waved me off, the shifter already perched on his lap. "I'll handle the tab, Dion."

First giving me sage advice, now offering to cover the bill? Who was this guy?

Heading outside, I flicked my collar from the brisk wind that'd picked up. It couldn't decide on a direction and had my long hair flying in flurries of darkness over my eyes. I'd walked three of the six blocks it took to reach the club, and a figure emerging from *Tobias's Smoke and Cigar Shop* gave me pause. Frustratingly, I slapped my hair from my gaze, focusing on the body—curvy, pale skin, *red* hair.

My heart throttled into a gallop before seizing for a beat in my chest.

Absently removing my phone, I typed up a quick message to Tambie.

Me

Close up for me tonight, will you?

Tambie

Seriously, boss? That'd be the fourth time this week.

Me

You can have tomorrow off.

Tambie

DONE.

Gulping, I slipped the phone back into my pocket and stared in front of me.

Chelsea fucking Stewart was in Arcane Cove, and she was mere meters away from me.

Four

Chelsea

A quaint bell sounded from the top of the wooden, white-washed door when I walked into the bakery. Scents of bread, vanilla, and cinnamon wafted through the air, already calming me. A center circular display with handwritten price placards harbored dozens of baked goods—muffins, bread loaves, cupcakes, and pastries. Toward the back was a domed, glass display case in front of the counter and cash register. Floor to ceiling stained glass windows, and an arched metal design with intricate patterns and foliage bordering it stood behind it.

"Sorry, sorry," a woman said from the back, hurrying to the counter while dusting her hands covered in flour. "You caught me in the middle of loading more loaves into the oven." Her hair was pulled back into a low ponytail, and she batted strands of her snowy blonde bangs from her eyes. She offered me a resplendent smile. "How can I help you?"

Snickering, I approached the counter and all but shoved my nose against the display case. "Don't suppose anything in here has the cure for self-pity?"

"I have just the thing," she responded in a sing-song tone.

My spine zipped straight, not expecting her to answer my joke so suddenly *or* seriously. The woman slid a door of the case to one side and, using wax paper, grabbed a chocolate cupcake covered in bright blue frosting, matching the blue hue her blonde hair trailed into at the tips. Her heart-shaped mouth matched the similar angle of her jaw, and when she looked at me again, I was in awe of her radiantly violet eyes.

"Here we are." She proudly rested the cupcake on a paper plate on the counter in front of me. "Chocolate hazelnut with blueberry frosting and—" Rubbing her fingers together above the dessert, shimmers of blue sparkles fell from seemingly nowhere, settling over the icing. "—a little magic." Her lush eyelashes caught on her bangs when she bounced in excitement, gauging my reaction.

"Is that glitter edible?" Dumbly, I pointed at the cupcake.

The woman's smile turned into a concerned frown, and she tilted her head to one side. "Of course, I—" Pausing, the grin slowly curved back onto her lips. "—you're new here, aren't you?"

"Is it that obvious?" My cheeks burned, and my Scottish heritage always made my skin flush pink from my face down to my neck.

A tender smile formed on the woman's plump lips, and she extended a hand. "I'm Sylvaria, but everyone calls me Sylvie."

"Chelsea." I shook Sylvie's hand, and when our skin made contact, a discomforting pang struck the back of my skull.

If I'd made a reactive face, Sylvie didn't notice or pay it any mind. She kept smiling and proceeded to put the cupcake in a small white bag. "Welcome to Arcane Cove, Chelsea." She held the bag out to me and wiggled it. "First one is on the house."

Blinking, because I couldn't have heard her right, I took the bag with a stiff arm. "I couldn't possibly. It's not a big deal. How much do I owe you?" I fished for my card in the tiny pockets of my yoga pants.

Sylvie waved her hands in the air while shaking her head, making her lusciously long blonde waves shift. "Nope. This one is on me, Chelsea. I'm sure you'll be in here again."

If it tasted nearly as good as this place smelled, for the sake of my ass and thighs, I'd have to forcibly *not* come here every dang day.

"In that case, then, thank you. Sincerely." Displaying the bag with a brightened smile, I backpedaled toward the door. "Have a good night."

Sylvie's eyes seemed to twinkle, not some glint from the candles, an actual *sparkle*. "You too."

Holding the bag with two fingers as if it were a stinky diaper versus a delectable treat, I stood on the sidewalk, eyeing the quiet streets. Most businesses were closed given the ungodly hour, but an establishment across the way still harbored a single flickering candle near its sign—*Tobias's Smoke & Cigar Shop*.

Chelsea, you shouldn't. Turn around and walk home. Just because it's conveniently open twenty-four hours like the bakery does not mean you need to go into it.

Despite the pep talk to myself, my flip-flops remain cemented. While staring at the shop, still debating on buying a pack of cigarettes, I decided to distract myself with a bite of cupcake. The precise moment the taste burst across my tongue felt akin to a surprise orgasm—the kind that sneaks up on you while doing crunches or when the male narrator of your audiobook hits that perfect decibel. I figured it would be a tasty treat, but the decadent flavors exploding in my mouth were enough to make me audibly gasp.

My shoulders relaxed, my mind cleared, and I instantly wished to feel more of it—all of it. So, I did what any other self-respecting woman with a deliriously amazing dessert would do—shoved the rest of it in until my cheeks puffed out like a greedy squirrel.

While chewing and resisting the urge to sexually moan on a public street corner, I became distracted once more by the quaint cigar shop.

"Screw it," I eventually decided because you know what? I'd been through a lot lately, and moving to an entirely new town where I didn't know a soul took a lot of guts. The likes of which I'd forgotten I possessed.

After crumbling the empty bag and tossing it in the rusted metal trash can, I whisked open the shop door, resonating another bell sound. This one hadn't been as pleasant sounding, in fact, it was irritatingly clanky at best.

"Hello," a man's voice chimed from somewhere. There were endless rows of cigars and rolled cigarettes displayed behind humidity-controlled glass. The back wall was entirely composed of pipes, cutters, and other smoking accessories.

Turning circles, I searched for the voice's source but saw nothing but merchandise. "Hello?"

A figure appeared over the counter piled high with boxes of overstock. He stood on a wooden rolling desk chair and adjusted his wire-rimmed glasses. His ears were more prominently rounded and stuck out from his head. Little hair was atop his head, but a thickly lined pair of mutton chops traveled from his temples down to his chin.

"Apologies. I don't often have that many customers at this time on a weekday morning. I was in the back room and hadn't heard you come in straight away." The man offered a warm smile, the bifocals he wore creating a fish-eye effect, making his eyes appear that much larger.

Waving him off, I walked further in, looking for a shelf with plain domestic cigarette boxes. "Not a problem. I'm honestly glad you were open."

"The name's Tobias. Are you looking for something in particular? Country of origin? Aromatic? Potion-laced?" Tobias slipped his thumbs under his burgundy suspenders and let them rest there.

Potion-laced?

"I'm afraid I'm not that well versed on cigars. I hoped to find a typical pack of menthols?" Suddenly feeling the size of a field mouse, I scratched the back of my head and averted my gaze.

Tobias laughed and snapped his suspenders. "Not to worry. I keep those behind the desk." He pulled open a drawer and placed the cigarette pack on the counter. "Will that be all for you?"

Tobias's overly jubilant demeanor wasn't fooling me. No doubt there was that little voice in the back of his head silently judging me and my poor taste.

"Yes. Will this cover it? You can keep the change." I'd rushed the words, slapping several bills on the table and waiting.

Tobias's eyes widened behind his glasses, and he slowly lifted the cash, using his short, wide fingers to comb through them. "My, my. I haven't seen this currency in quite a long time." He snapped his gaze to me over the rim of his spectacles. "Where are you from, dearie?"

This *currency? Was I not still in America?*

"Moved here a few days ago." Flashing a quick grin, I swiped the cigarettes into my palm. "Thank you."

Tobias chuckled, the sound of an old-school cash register's drawer chiming open the last thing I heard before making it back to the reprieve of the sidewalk. Sighing, I pressed my back to the building's brick wall and fumbled with the wrapping on the pack. Flicking a single cigarette from it and resting it between my lips, I felt my pockets for the small lighter I'd always kept there.

Ugh. There were barely any pockets in these flipping yoga pants, let alone big enough to store a flipping lighter.

Something heavy pressed into my palm on the underside of the pack. Eyeing my hand warily, I turned it over to reveal a bright red lighter. I glanced around as if someone had managed to sneak it into my grasp without looking. Deciding that Tobias included it, I raised it to the cigarette, lit it, and took a few puffs. It irritated me how quickly one singular drag of a cigarette could relieve my rattled nerves and stress. I wanted to quit, I honestly did, but the results were hard to ignore.

It's when I opened my eyes that the nerves and borderline panic quickly returned. At first, I thought my vision was playing some cruel joke on me, but there was no mistaking that salty beach-wavy dark hair or the massive height of packed muscle. Dion. He was *here*.

"Chelsea?" Dion said, standing several feet from me with about as befuddled of an expression as I'm sure was plastered on my face. His gaze shifted to the cigarette smoke curling in the air by my head.

Yelping, I threw the cigarette at my feet and stomped it with my sandal. "Dion, fancy uh—fancy running into you."

It wasn't until Dion edged closer that pure terror wrung my bones. He'd never seen me like this—unkept and flustered. I had zero make-up on, my hair was as flat as an ironing board, and I wore *flip-flops*. Not to mention, he'd seen me smoking now.

"Yeah." Dion stepped toward me like an Irwin approaching a hungry crocodile. "What are you doing in the Cove?"

Folding my arms around myself and readjusting my posture to appear at least somewhat attractive, I flicked my hair behind me. "I live here."

Dion's eyes did that damn twinkle that I couldn't recall ever failing to make my knees wobbly. "Is that so?" A grin tugged at his lips, and his gaze unabashedly roamed my yoga pants, my hair and landed on my face.

"Yup. Right there, in fact." I pointed at my apartment building behind him.

He glanced over his shoulder, rubbed his chin, and chuckled with that deep-as-sin voice of his. "I'll be damned. I live two blocks that way off Sycamore." Dion jutted his thumb behind me.

Sand coated my throat, and I dragged my nails over my neck. "Wow. That's uh—that's close."

"Sure is," Dion responded, his husky voice louder now from having stepped within a breath's reach of me.

Sucking in a quick breath, not because he startled me, but because of the way his scent ignited my core within a heartbeat, I stared at him.

"If you moved here, what happened to your clients?" Dion slipped his hands in his pockets, those dark eyes still taking me in.

Despite my best efforts, I could feel my feet going pigeon-toed, and it may have been the only thing keeping me from collapsing. "Warm transferred to other specialists. After Harm retired, I didn't see a point in sticking around and sought greener pastures."

"And you settled on the Cove?" Dion's brows did that skin-pinching quirking I remembered when he was especially curious about something.

I continued to rub my neck, undoubtedly making it red. "I don't know how to describe it other than it sung to me. Is that crazy?"

"Not crazy, Red. Not in the slightest." He smiled again, tilting his head to one side. "Look at you. Moved away from your comfort zone, are out in public without any make-up, you smoke, and you have blue icing on your cheek."

"I—what?" Wiping my hand over the same side Dion pointed, I grimaced at the blue stain smearing my palm. And Tobias couldn't have done me a solid and warned me in the shop? "Dammit," I said under my breath.

"And you're swearing?" Dion leaned back, his hands still in his pockets, and a roar of laughter burst from his chest. "Fuck, Chels. This place is doing you some good, huh?"

One could say that. One could also say it led me back to *him*. And that realization was about as terrifying as it was invigorating.

Not answering him, I kept wiping my hand over that spot on my face, thinking I hadn't gotten it all.

"Listen, Stewart. I'm sure this will come as a shock to you, but I pretty much know everyone in town, and I happen to excel at socializing." Dion pressed a hand to his chest and bowed.

Whenever he referred to me by my last name in the past suggested he meant business.

"You don't say," I mused with extra sarcasm and a grin that I couldn't stop if I tried.

"Why don't I introduce you to some potential clients? Save you the leg work."

The urge to fidget suddenly overwhelmed me. "You'd do that?"

Dion guffawed and uncomfortably rubbed the back of his neck. "Damn. The way you said it makes me sound like an asshole."

"I didn't mean it like that. I just—" I reached a hand toward him before I had the chance to think about my actions. Dion wore a jacket, but a spark still sizzled from our contact the moment my fingers rested on the fabric. Gulping, I let my touch slip away, harboring that pleasantly surprised expression he gave. "—that's a huge ask. What would you want in return?"

"Sex," Dion clipped without hesitation.

My cheeks flushed, and my stomach sprung into erratic somersaults at the mere thought of it with him—with the Greek god of wine and—

"I'm kidding," he added, bending his knees to look me in the eye. "Unless it's on the table."

I threw him an exasperated glare and said nothing because I couldn't trust myself with words. Given the butterflies dancing in my stomach, I may have taken him up on it.

"Right," Dion said, smirking. "Look. Don't worry about it. It's very much in my wheelhouse and not a big deal."

Combing some hair over my ear, I felt my cheeks blush again, but for an entirely different reason. "Dion, you know I can't without—"

"Okay, fine," Dion interrupted, waiting for me to lift my gaze back to his face. "A date then."

The butterflies turned into hummingbirds. "A *date*?"

"Yup. Just a date." Dion leaned his shoulder on the streetlamp situated between us. "No preconceived expectations. Just us."

Us.

Any woman in their right mind would've already answered him with a resounding "fuck yes," but if I was being honest with myself, Dion put me on edge. It wasn't because I worried about him hurting me in a physical sense, but the emotional side? Well, he hadn't exactly kept the best track record.

Then again, Harm was rooting for us. She'd already confessed that to me weeks ago. And if he did hurt me? He'd have two war gods to contend with. It was enough reassurance.

"Alright, fine." I leaned on the same pole and lifted my nose into the air like this was a typical business transaction.

"Great. I'll pick you up tomorrow." Dion bit his lower lip, his brows bobbing.

Pushing from the pole, I eyed him warily. "Tomorrow? You haven't introduced me to any clients yet."

Dion winked at me before briefly, ever so fleetingly, cupping my chin with his thumb and forefinger. "I'll have you meet six tomorrow during the day, and by night, we'll go on our date. Yeah?"

The confidence swarming this man in absolute *spades.*

"I—" Words again failed me, and I slapped a palm to my forehead. "—sure."

"It's settled then." Dion snapped his fingers, a new form of hitch in his giddy-up as he started to walk past me in the direction of his home. "Oh, and Chels—"

Here it was—some clandestine confession or explanation as to why he took so long to text me.

"You might want to use some soap on that." He pointed to his cheek where the previous icing had been on mine. "Looks like it stained your skin blue."

Mortification consumed me, and I fought the compulsion to lift the collar of my shirt over my face. "Will do, see you tomorrow." I rushed the words before I power walked toward my building.

"I'm super stoked to have run into you, Red," Dion shouted after me with his hands cupped around his mouth.

Given it was three in the morning, I looked for a light turning on from one of the apartment windows, yelling at us to pipe down. Not answering him, I pointed to myself and then held up two fingers.

Dion chuckled, used his thumb to scratch his chin, and turned on his heel with his hands in his pockets.

And here we had it. I was about to let Dionysus, a Greek god, attempt to seduce me. I knew it. He knew it. And now, there wasn't any more beating around the bush over it. But there was too much fun still to be had before letting myself fully succumb to his charm. That is—if I could *help* myself.

Five

I'd walked home in an actual fucking daze. Not only had I miraculously run into Chelsea Stewart, but I'd run into her *in* Arcane Cove. It took every ounce of restraint in my godly arsenal not to physically let my jaw drop to the floor to move past the initial shock of seeing her in the flesh again. The dawning realization that if she was here, the wards allowed her to pass through—defensive wards placed by sorcerers and warlocks. They shielded the Cove like an invisible dome to prevent any non-magical beings from finding the hidden sanctuary.

It begged the question—what was she then? A nymph? Nah, she was far too reserved. A sprite? Too tall. There was the possibility of a faerie, but as spellbinding as Chelsea's jade eyes were, they weren't that uncommon of a color.

Then I'd catapulted into a panic—me, Dionysus, the most laid-back god of them all—*panicked* over how I was going to see her again as fast as inhumanly possible. But I'd always been one to think quickly on my feet, and work is something that never left Red's mind. I'd offered to help her for *her* betterment, sure, but it also selfishly gave me the juiciest of excuses to be around her all. Damn. Day.

I'd been so lost in my thoughts that I hadn't seen Bruce lying on the steps leading to my building's entrance. Then again, stairs weren't a typical place where one chose to take a nap. I lifted my booted foot, glaring down at the grumbling satyr who I often called my friend and occasional assistant.

"Bruce, what the Tartarus are you doing outside my building? Did you get drunk at the pixie party again?" When he only answered with more grunting, I lightly shoved my boot into his portly stomach.

Bruce giggled like the Pillsbury Doughboy, rubbing his vest-covered stomach, his hooved feet curling upward. He wrapped a finger around one of his small horns sprouting from the front of his skull covered in a thick mass of dark brown hair, still happily sleeping away and not waking up.

Sighing, I snapped my fingers, producing a chalice of water, and poured it over Bruce's head.

Bruce screeched, sputtered, and clamored to stand, holding both fists in the air as if he were ready to fight whoever attempted to drown him. "I know I don't look like much, but I—" He blinked when he spotted me and lowered his hands. "Boss. Didn't see you there."

"How could you? You were passed out on the stairs." Brushing past him, I fluttered my burgundy magic as a pin code and paused with the door half ajar once I heard Bruce's hooves scraping the concrete behind me.

Bruce slipped his hairy arms behind his back, dragging the point of one hoof back and forth in front of him. "Don't suppose you'd find it in your good graces to let me crash on your couch until I sleep this off?"

"I thought we talked about this." Leaning on the doorframe, I hung my thumb through a belt loop. "Remember what I said?"

Bruce wrapped a hand around each horn, clenching them for support. "That it was the last time you'd sort out my mistake if I got carried away at the pixie party again."

"That's right. Are you making me out to be a liar?" The skin beneath my eye twitched because I bit the inside of my cheek so harshly to keep from cracking my demeanor.

Bruce's eyes went wide as harvest moons, and he clip-clopped several times. "No, sir, not at all. It'll never happen again. Cross my heart and hope for some pie."

I rolled my eyes at my sad excuse for an assistant, not bothering to correct him. "Shut up, you old goat. We both know that's not true. And what kind of god of debauchery would I be to look down on partying so hard you passed out on concrete stairs?"

Bruce perked up at that, his small, bushy tail swaying in delight. "Does that mean you'll let me in?"

Not answering, I pushed open the door but blocked him with my leg before he entered. "This is the last time, though, Bruce. You get drunk off your ass as much as you want with the pixies so long as it doesn't interfere with your work. And next time, because there *will* be many more times, you bother Selene at the inn instead. Understood?"

"Crystalline clear, boss," Bruce answered, saluting me.

"What are you doing?"

"Saluting you, sir. Captain." Bruce squinted one eye, which meant he was desperately trying not to see double.

Growling, I yanked him inside. "For fuck's sake, get in here."

Usually, I'd opt to take the stairs as an act of normalcy, but I sure as shit wasn't going to carry Bruce's sorry ass up them, so I coaxed him into the elevator—still normal enough, probably more so. As it ascended to the top floor, I crossed my arms and leaned against the wall, propping Bruce up with one foot, grimacing at the drool dripping from his mouth and gathering in a puddle at his hooves.

Once the doors binged open and I gave Bruce a nudge, we eventually made it into my loft apartment, and Bruce begrudgingly crawled to my black leather couch facing the wall of windows. The satyr pawed at one of four satin, wine-colored pillows on the couch and stuffed it under his head after combing his beard with his fingers.

"Say, boss, why were you out so late, huh? I thought you normally got in around one thirty?" Bruce asked, his eyes already growing heavy.

I'd made a beeline for the kitchen, strolling past one of four ceiling-to-floor wooden wine racks I owned filled with varieties of wine, some dating back to early Earth years in the seventeen hundreds. Grabbing a random bottle, I yanked the cork out with my teeth and flipped a glass with pewter ivy swirling up its stem onto the countertop.

"Chelsea," I answered, not stopping the pour until it reached the brim but didn't overflow.

Bruce's head appeared over the top of the couch and he suddenly sobered. "The red-headed broad?"

"Hey—" I grabbed an entire vine of grapes from a wooden bowl and hurled them at him, smacking him square in the forehead. "—

don't call her that."

After Bruce sputtered, he raised his hands in defeat. "Alright, alright. But is that who you're talking 'bout? The one you been texting and pining over?" A sly grin creased Bruce's lips, and he rested his chin on his arm, supported on the couch's back.

"She lives in the Cove now," I continued, propping my ass against the back counter and slurping a quarter of the wine.

Bruce nodded until reaching the same epiphany I had, his chin lifting. "Wait. I thought she was human."

"Me too. Clearly, she's not." I grumbled the last words and ran my fingertip over the grooved designs of the metal leaves on the drink's cup.

Bruce scratched the back of his ear with a hoof like a damn animal, making me wince from fear he had fleas. "You make it sound like a bad thing."

We'd been worlds apart before we knew of each other's existence. When we met, she'd already been introduced to the magical world of myths and gods I hailed from, which had been far more a breath of fresh air than I could've predicted. Now, I've learned she *was* a part of my world.

"No, Bruce." Guzzling more wine, I flashed him a toothy smile. "This is fucking *great*."

Six

Chelsea

The next day, I awoke from the strangest dream. One would think it'd have been of the scandalous variety with a specific wine god, but it was me staring out my apartment window from such an incredibly odd angle. It was as if I was leaning my head on the armrest of the couch or something. My head motions were also weird because I moved so suddenly and erratically. When I opened my eyes, I stretched my limbs into a star beneath my comfy pale green comforter and yawned.

Riley was perched on the couch's armrest staring out the—I sat up and stared at my pet ferret. He was staring out the same window I'd dreamt about. How was that possible? He suddenly turned circles, his nose twitching, and abruptly stopped pointing out the window with his elongated body.

"Chelsea," Dion yelled from outside.

He'd said we would get started this morning, but why would he be here this early? Glancing at the digital clock on my nightstand did nothing for my cause. I'd slept in. Really slept in. It was almost ten thirty. I couldn't recall a time I'd *ever* slept this late.

"Oh, Red," Dion beckoned again, louder this time. "I'm going to keep embarrassing you until you acknowledge my presence." He'd drawn out the first "e," and by the tilt in his voice, I could tell he grinned through it all.

Biting back a smile, I scrambled from my bed and knelt on the couch, unlocking the window and pushing it open. Dion stood on the sidewalk in front of my building, clad in his usual combat boots, military jacket, torn dark jeans, and tightly ribbed tank top. I clenched my thighs together and leaned my forearms on the sill. "Didn't think to knock on my door?"

"How could I?" Dion shielded his eyes with a hand from the sun. "I didn't know which one was yours."

Tapping my hands on the wood, I leaned out further, half my body through the window now. "I thought a man of your—" I paused, knowing most of the building and anyone passing by could hear us, and I didn't want to blow his cover. "—caliber would have a way to tell?"

Dion scrunched his nose like he'd gotten a whiff of minotaur shit. "Like how?"

"I don't know. X-ray vision? Like Superman?" It took everything in me not to sway my hips like a teeny bopper with a crush on a rock star with what this man did to me. And here I was again with zero make-up, and I couldn't care less.

Dion laughed and shook his head. "Trust me. No one wants *me* with that kind of power. You comin' down, or do I have to fireman carry you out of there?"

My stomach flipped over itself at that, and I tightly gripped the window's molding. "Give me five minutes."

Dion nodded as if he didn't believe me. "So, in female code, does that mean an hour?"

"What?" I feigned shock, pressing a hand to my chest. His gaze zeroed in on the placement instantaneously. "Alright, thirty minutes tops. Do you want to wait inside?"

The words flew from my mouth before I had a chance to think about the implications of such a simple question rationally.

Dion's hand dropped, and he arched a thickly sculpted brow. "In your apartment?"

I knew inviting him in was playing with fire, but it'd been so long since I took risks. Nodding, I lifted my chin. "Yeah. As long as you can grab the door in time for me to buzz you in. Three, two—" Not giving him another part of the countdown, I dashed for the buzzer, all out *giggling* as I went and hit the button. The lower-toned sound indicating the street door had been opened resonated, and I *swooned* over a freaking door.

My heart raced as I waited for him to reach my apartment, my hands clasped under my chin. The deep thuds of his booted, heavy steps echoed down the hallway until they stopped, and his knuckles knocking on my door replaced it. "It's me, Red."

Pressing my eye to the peephole, I yelped when his face, distorted by the fisheye effect, stared back at me. "You'll have to specify who *me* is, I'm afraid."

"You do know I can still get in there with the door locked?"

"Let me get this straight. You can't see through walls, but you can penetrate them?" Of all the words I could've chosen. Penetrate? I rubbed my feet together like a cricket.

Dion pressed his hands on each side of the peephole and flashed me a wicked grin. "You want to see me break the door down, don't you? That part of your hidden kink, Chelsea?"

My skin flushing, I immediately unlocked and opened the door, sending both our hair in winded plumes.

He was leaning on the doorframe. *Leaning.* It wasn't even the least bit fair. "Hey."

"Hey, yourself," I replied, peeling wood grains from my side of the door with a nail.

"You asked me up here, Red. You gonna invite me in?" Dion's caramel eyes lifted behind me, trying to peer into my apartment.

Suddenly feeling exposed despite being fully clothed, I closed the door enough for him to only to see my face. "That depends. Are you going to try to have your way with me?"

Dion chuckled—deep, masculine, and a pure carnal hymn. "Have my way with you, Chels? You're worried about me trying to *fuck* you?"

It was more about the worry of me climbing him like a damn redwood at this point. Could I trust *myself* with him in my personal space?

When I didn't answer straight away, Dion hovered his face near mine. "Is it because you're afraid you'd let me? Because you *want* to?" His gaze lowered to my lips at those last words.

His scent infiltrated my senses—wine, soap, and a little earthy. "That's hardly fair, D. You know the essence you give off to mortal women. Why do you think I restricted us to texting this entire time?"

The smile on Dion's face turned predatory. "Why not let go a little, Stewart? See where being impulsive takes you, hm?"

I'd sensed my growing attraction for him from the moment he'd waltzed into my life, and it only grew with each passing conversation via written word alone. But now, seeing him again after all this time, after the flirting and the pining, there was a pull—a delicious tug on my bones and soul—and it terrified me.

"Letting go around you, Dionysus is like stepping into the path of a tornado with your arms spread." I'd breathed out the words, my gaze unabashedly roaming his chiseled jawline and his taut, muscular torso hiding behind that tank top.

"That's the thing about tornadoes, though—" Dion shifted some of the hair that fell into my eyes. His fingertip ever so lightly brushed my cheek, and the contact was like a lightning strike to my skin. "They're unpredictable and just might surprise you."

Leaning further into him because I could not help my damn self, I slowly closed my eyes, my lips parting—

A tiny growl sounded from behind me.

"Is that a *ferret?*" Dion asked, his mouth lingering near mine, but his gaze had shifted over my shoulder.

Riley stood on his hind legs, growling and hissing, his paws batting the air in front of him as if he intended to swat Dion with them.

Sighing, I pushed open the door, the mood officially squelched by my pet ferret. He'd undoubtedly done me a favor, so I couldn't be that mad at him for it. "It is. You're not allergic or anything, are you?"

Dion gave me a look that suggested I should have rethought my question.

"Right. Come on in," I said, breezing him through the doorway with a flourish.

Dion went from a burly, macho man to a cooing animal lover within breath's reach of Riley. He hunched forward, resting his palms on the tops of his thighs. "Hey there, little guy. I'm Dion.

Not a threat to your mama, I promise."

Riley gave a final hiss before he hesitantly sniffed Dion's offered arm. After several circles, another sniff or two, and multiple gropes with his paws, my ferret deemed Dion trustworthy and spiraled up his arm, resting in the crook of it.

"Okay, he's fucking adorable. What's his name?" Dion chuckled and used a single finger to scratch Riley's head.

"Riley." I crossed my arms and watched as a Greek god won over my ferret's heart within seconds. Most beings would *never* manage to win his affection.

"How'd you find him?"

Leaving those two to get further acquainted, I moved to the bathroom to primp. "Funny enough, he found *me*."

Dion didn't answer right away. "Huh. That *is* funny. What do you mean exactly?"

"It was the strangest thing because I went for a run on one of those wooded trails that used to be by me in Colorado. He scampered from the trees and stood on the path on his hind legs. It was like he demanded my attention." Laughing, I put curlers in my hair and started on my make-up.

"You don't say," Dion responded—distant and thoughtful.

With only one eye done up, I leaned from the doorway with a narrowed gaze. "Why did you say it like that?"

Dion appeared in deep thought but snapped to attention and plastered a wide smile. "No reason. Just listening."

Studying him for a minute longer, I acquiesced and dipped back into the bathroom. "Anyway, something compelled me to take him in, so I adopted him, and the rest is history. He's been my best bud ever since. Well, besides my sister and Harm."

Dion guffawed. "Preferring non-animals to be superior friends? How barbaric."

"Shut up," I replied through a smile, my voice distorted from applying mascara. "So, who are you introducing me to? I have to say, I'm pretty curious."

"About that, Red," Dion said, his voice louder and closer from standing in the bathroom doorway, my ferret still curled within his arm.

After sucking in a quick breath and dropping the make-up wand, I turned and held onto the sink behind me for dear life.

"I want to make you a deal." Dion's gaze focused on the curlers in my hair, a warm smile edging his lips.

My grip tightened on the marble from his proximity, but gods help me, I loved every moment of it. "A deal?"

"I'm going to introduce you to a single client to start, and if they agree to sign on, we go on that date early and continue tomorrow." Dion's eyes pinned mine, a sort of hopeful plea resonating there.

He was certainly up to something, and it only made me more curious.

"This must be a pretty prestigious client. What do they do?" My shoulders relaxed, and instead of pressing into the sink, I rested on it.

Dion's jaw tightened, and his gaze turned to the ceiling before landing back on me. "He's a *rock star*."

A rock star? That could be huge for me—for my career.

"A *mythical* one," he added, enticing a smile from me that could have put the sun's brightness to shame.

Seven

Hermes was going to have a fucking field day with this one. Not only was he right about Apollo, but I bit back my pride to do it for *her*. I'm tempted to avoid him at all costs for the foreseeable future, but that often proved difficult with someone who can run at the speed of light. I knew Apollo would jump at the chance to have a PR manager like Chelsea because she wasn't human—a small fact *she* wasn't aware of yet and more of the reason to hurry this shit along. More and more hints about what she was kept piling up, and I knew I needed to tell her as soon as possible.

The sooner she knew, the sooner we could navigate it together. At least, I hoped it would happen that way. Chelsea never seemed the type to have freak-outs, but this was entirely new territory for her *and* me. The way I figured, it'd go one of two ways. One, she'd be shocked at first but soon settle into curiosity and excitement. Two, she'd call me a liar or something, storm off, and move back to the human world ignoring any of her magical abilities.

I wished with every ounce of my unnatural power for the former possibility.

The way her eyes had glistened at the mention of him being a rock star gave me a peculiar tingling sensation in my chest. Her happiness breathed new life into me, and now all I could think about was continually making that expression appear on her. To make her happy had become a new intoxicating, addictive drug.

Forty minutes had gone by, and she was still locked away in the bathroom. A nagging itch at the base of my spine—the feral variety—made me jealous and protective when I thought about her going to all this trouble for my shit-eating half-brother and not *me*. But that was the beast in me talking. The other, the more laid-back side of me, recognized the stolen glances and smiles she gave me when she thought I wasn't looking.

Chelsea's ferret Riley curled up in a ball in the crook of my arm and slept, the tiniest of snores I'd ever heard escaping his throat. She called him a pet, but I had the gut feeling he was far more than that. I busied myself snooping around the apartment while I waited, a dopey grin plastered on my face from how much every square inch broadcast her personality. But other things, like the several unpacked boxes, surprised me. She'd always seemed so well-kept, down to the way she folded her jacket and neatly placed it on the back of her chair before sitting.

She did, however, take the time to hang a singular item on the wall above her desk—a framed ABBA vinyl record. Specifically, a red heart-shaped one with the band posed together in a photo at the center.

"Do you like ABBA?" Chelsea asked, appearing at my side the way I'd met her the first time—a black designer jacket pressed to perfection and a matching skirt, black pumps that were undoubtedly red on the bottom, and an emerald button-up shirt.

Her hair fell in pristine waves over her shoulders, and my gaze dropped to her plump, glossed lips.

Smirking, I offered a still-slumbering Riley to her. "Doesn't everyone? I don't recognize this album, though."

Considering the heart shape, I could've made an easy guess what song was on the label on the other side, but I wanted her to *tell* me.

After Chelsea secured Riley in his carpeted tower, she sauntered back to the framed album and, despite it not being crooked, adjusted the corners. She rested her hands on her hips and gave a wistful sigh. "It's a special Valentine's edition with *Lay All Your Love on Me* on it."

I caught myself staring at her profile—the way her nose did an elaborate swoosh from the bridge to the tip. Fucking adorable. "Oh, yeah? That your favorite song of theirs?"

"You have no idea," she breathed out. She snapped her attention to me, and I forced my gaze away from the exposed cleavage, given the three buttons undone. "You ready to go?"

"Yeah. He said he'd meet us at *Prancing Pegasus*. It's a diner. That cool with you?" Slipping my phone from my back pocket, I checked my text message to ensure I had the time correct.

Chelsea shrugged and snatched her tan purse resting on the desk. "Sure. I can schmooze just about anywhere." A confident smile graced her lips, and the sight of it made me want to wrap my hand around the back of her neck, pull her to me, and finish what we'd started at her doorway earlier.

"I bet you can. Think this is the first time I'll get to witness the *magic*, so to speak, huh?" Walking to the door, I held it open for her.

"It isn't magic, Dion, just experience," she responded, her eyes sparking to life as she got into publicist mode.

Or it *was* magic. Time will tell.

We'd ordered coffee and slunk into a corner booth at the back of the diner. I opted to sit on the same side as her because I sure as shit didn't want Apollo *that* close to her. Chelsea had her hands wrapped around her mug, her fingernails rhythmically tapping against it. Her gaze was fixed on the door, and if she had an ounce of nervousness about her, she didn't show it.

My phone buzzed, and I lifted the screen, peeking at the preview of a text message.

Dick Head

I'm here.

Sighing and resting my phone back down, I nudged Chelsea's arm. "He's here."

"Wait, are you two on texting terms? Is this someone you know personally?" Chelsea's eyes lit up, undoubtedly piecing it together bit by bit. She knew I was a Greek god with a huge family.

I'd have answered her, but the sound of the door chiming garnered her attention, and her hands flattened on the table. "Dion, is that Ace? As in *Apollo* of Apollo's Suns?"

Fuck me.

"You know that band?" I flippantly asked.

Chelsea zipped her spine straight and quickly combed her fingers through her hair. "I'm a woman. Of course, I do."

Of course, she did.

"Dion," Apollo shouted from the entrance, waving at us with an emphatic raised hand. His ridiculously white teeth glinted when he smiled, grabbing the attention of the three other customers in the restaurant.

Rolling my eyes, I slouched in the seat, pretending for the moment that I didn't know him.

Chelsea stood and tugged on the bottom of her jacket, immediately extending a hand once Apollo approached us. "Ace, it's an honor to meet you and even more of an honor that you're considering me as your publicist."

The smile had yet to fade from Apollo's tanned face. He tossed some of that light blonde mop on his head that he called hair from his eyes before shaking her hand. "Pleasure is all mine, Miss Stewart. Dion here had nothing but good things to say about you. And you can call me Apollo. We're all family here, right?" Apollo winked at me before taking a seat across from us.

I fought every compulsion not to kick his shin underneath the table.

"I—alright. I guess you *are* aware of my ties with your brothers and knowing their *true* selves, huh?" Chelsea sat and removed an e-tablet from her purse, quickly inputting the PIN code to unlock the screen.

Apollo drummed his fingers on the table before rubbing the sun pendant hanging to his chest between two fingers. He looked like he'd just come from a damn concert wearing only a metallic gold vest and fucking leather pants. "And your sister, right?"

Chelsea perked up. "That's right." She laughed and opened a screen with typed-up notes. "I'm sure you're a very busy man, Apollo, so I don't wish to keep you long, but I did have one question."

"Only one?" Apollo stretched his arms over the booth's back, and he kept glancing between me and Chelsea, still grinning.

"I figured a musician of your caliber would already have a publicist?"

Apollo nodded. "I did and unfortunately had to let him go last week."

Chelsea's fingers flew as she typed on the touch screen. "I'm sorry to hear that. May I ask why?"

"I guess I came to realize that someone like me—what I am—needed more of a—" Apollo waved his hands around, his bottom lip sticking out like he was thinking of the proper word. "—special touch."

Heat prickled my neck, and I sat forward, pressing my elbows into the table so harshly I dented it.

"Special? Oh, you mean you prefer having a female publicist?"

Apollo chuckled, gave me a glance, and continued. "No, no. That doesn't matter. What I guess I meant was I need someone more—*magical.*"

And now I did kick him under the table, a growl bubbling at the back of my throat.

Apollo grunted, smiled, and tapped his forehead where my horns normally protruded.

"Magical?" Chelsea laughed, bubbly and bright. "I guess you *could* compare what publicists do to performing miracles."

Apollo rested his chin on his hand. "Precisely. And I've heard you're one of the *best* miracle workers."

"I'm flattered, thank you." Chelsea re-positioned on her seat, crossing her legs beneath the table and sitting with perfect posture. "What all do you expect from a publicist?"

Apollo squinted his blue eyes at the ceiling before answering. "I suppose the biggest concern is keeping my identity hidden from the general public."

There was no stopping the snort that blurted from my mouth. For someone so concerned about blowing his cover, one would think he wouldn't display his powers during every fucking concert.

Chelsea glanced at me, giving me a pinched smile. Like a silently chastised canine, I sat up, prepared to zip my mouth for the duration of the conversation.

"That's completely understandable, and your confidentiality would be my top priority, I assure you. What else?" Chelsea continued to type and paused, lifting her gleaming eyes back to Apollo.

"As long as you make me look good, Miss Stewart, I'm a pretty easy man to please." Apollo winked at her, a spark flashing in his right eye.

The front of my skull ached, the horns trying to force themselves out. Balling my hand into a fist and resting it on my lap, I tempered the beast down.

"Absolutely. I'd be happy to give you contact information for former clients who agreed to speak on my behalf if you wish."

Apollo flicked his wrist. "Not necessary. You're already coming with glowing recommendations."

Chelsea's cheeks turned rosy.

"And say, Dion, does this also mean you got my reply to your wanted ad? The one looking for performances for your club?" Apollo swayed his hand back and forth like he was conducting an orchestra.

This son of a bitch.

"You own a club?" Chelsea asked, curiosity lacing her tone but also a hint of hurt that made my stomach clench.

Giving a quick nod, I stayed focused on my idiot half-brother. "Are you signing on with her or not, Apollo?"

"Oh, there's no need to rush." Chelsea pressed a hand over my bicep, and the contact made my entire body feel like melting wax. I couldn't say I'd ever felt so *relaxed* before.

"No point in dragging it out, Miss Stewart. You're hired." Apollo offered his hand again, and they shook, Chelsea's eyes beaming. "Where do I sign?"

"Give me one moment," Chelsea replied, excitedly swiping through screens on her tablet before turning it around and sliding it toward Apollo. "If you don't want to use your finger, I have a—"

Apollo signed his name with a flourish of his index finger and flipped the tablet back to her.

"—stylus," Chelsea finished, pulling it from her purse and staring gobsmacked at the signature. "You didn't want to read through the contract first?"

Apollo beat his fingers on the table before pushing to his feet. "No need. I trust you."

Chelsea rubbed her collarbones, causing her skin to redden. "Well, thank you. I should give you my cell number before you leave."

Apollo slipped his hands in his pockets. "Dion has my number; you can text it to me. Right, bro?"

"I'll give it to her. Shouldn't *you* be getting back to New York?" I'd said it through gritted teeth, unsure how much longer I could hold back from sucker-punching him in the jaw.

Apollo pressed his palms together and bowed. "Guilty as charged. But text me, Chelsea, and we'll set a meeting up next week to iron everything out, yeah?"

"Perfect." Chelsea rose and shook Apollo's hand. "Thank you again."

Apollo turned and headed for the exit right as an ogre entered the diner. His skin was a pale green,with two large curved tusks sticking out from his bottom lip. He had to duck to fit through the doorway. I sprung to action, purposely scooting past Chelsea and moving to the spot across from her, keeping her attention away from the obvious before I had a chance to tell her.

And that time was *now*.

Eight

Chelsea

Laughing at Dion playing musical chairs, I playfully shoved his shoulder. "What are you doing?"

"Going on a date with you." Dion pointed down, beckoning me to sit.

Slowly, I obliged, sinking to my seat and eyeing him warily. "Here? Right now?"

"Why not? This place has the best burgers in town." Dion raised his arm and turned his attention to the man behind the counter. "Marty, two specials, one with extra mustard and a chocolate milkshake, would ya?"

"You got it, D," the man replied gruffly.

Powering off the tablet, I slipped it into my purse and folded my hands on the table. "I love chocolate milkshakes."

"I know." Dion grinned and pressed his forearms to the table, bringing his sultry stare closer to me.

I'd taken a moment to appreciate how different from Apollo he looked sitting across from me. Dion carried himself differently. Apollo was clearly an attractive man, but Dion had a sort of feral energy about him—his sexy, unkempt hair, the beard, the tattoos. If I hadn't known any better, I'd label him as one of those shifters in a paranormal romance novel—the alpha kind who became crazed to claim their mates and mark them as theirs. The thought made my core tighten.

"Did I tell you that at some point?" I rubbed my thumbs together.

Dion chuckled and finger-walked across the table until his rough terra cotta hand found mine, and he grazed my skin. "You did. I believe it was a random text at two in the morning saying that you could really go for a chocolate milkshake right about now."

Heat pooled in my face, and I slapped a hand over my eyes. "Ugh. The things I've felt compelled to text you these past few months."

Dion's fingers brushed my knuckles, and he gently lowered my hand. "And I've felt privileged to receive every one of them, Chels." He pinned me with his gaze, my ass melting into the seat and ever so slowly, then brought my knuckles to his mouth, kissing my skin.

A raspy breath escaped my throat, and I nibbled my lip.

"There's something I need to tell you, and it may come as a bit of a shock, but all I'm asking is for you to keep an open mind. Alright?" Dion caressed my hand with his bottom lip, back and forth, all while keeping his eyes focused on mine.

Such an ominous introduction should've made me far more worried to hear what he had to say. Between the strokes from his lips against my knuckles and the lust and intrigue dancing circles in his dark eyes, he could've told me the world was ending tomorrow, and I couldn't say I'd panic about it.

"Okay," I whispered, offering him a reassuring smile.

He lowered our hands to the table and held out an open palm

to take both of mine with his. "That's my girl."

His girl. What I wouldn't give to have that label, and yet I'd stupidly fought it all this time.

"What's up, Dion? You can tell me anything." I squeezed his hands.

Dion made languid strokes on the tops of my hands with his calloused thumbs. "Take a look around you, Red. And I mean really look. Tell me what you see."

If any other person had asked me to do the same thing, I would've paused to ask the why of it before succumbing, but not with Dion. He'd always been my singular act of impulsivity until I decided to up and move to Arcane Cove. Thinking back on it, though, I'd say part of that was a little voice in my head telling me to just fucking do it—Dion's voice.

Clearing my throat, I sat up straight and pivoted around the diner. "I see tables, chairs, and windows. A young couple in the opposite corner from us, both with long, straight hair. One has—" I paused after taking in the details. "—pointed ears." Confusion pulled my glance to Dion to confirm it, and he gave a reassuring nod to continue. "Um, an older woman is sitting by herself reading a book, and sitting at the bar is a man with—" Staring at him at first, I gulped. "—green skin and tusks? Dion, what—"

Dion tightened his grip on my hands and pulled me toward him, my elbows sliding across the table. "Think about it. That couple in the corner? Elves. The older woman? A banshee. The green fellow? An ogre. The owner here, Marty? He's a walrus shifter. A Greek god is sitting across from you, and another just signed on to be your client."

When I tried to sit back, Dion held on tighter and wouldn't

let me budge, grounding me. The bakery shop owner—when she said she sprinkled it with magic—she *meant* it.

"So, what are you trying to say? This place? The Cove? It's full of mythical, magical beings?" I clenched my knees together under the table to keep them from bouncing.

"Yes, and *no* humans. There are wards guarding this place that don't allow them entry." Dion said the last few words slower and more deliberately.

My breathing grew shallow, and my heartbeat throttled into a gallop. "Then how did I get—" A tightness coiled in my throat, and I suddenly couldn't blink. "Oh," I breathed out. "*Oh.*"

"Oh," Dion repeated, tilting his head to the side to study me.

"Oh, gods. Oh my—" Confusion spiraled through me like a cyclone.

Dion bolted from his seat and sat next to me, his massive arm wrapping my shoulders, hands rubbing up and down my arms. "Breathe, Chels. Breathe."

My efforts at taking deep breaths turned into my cheeks puffing like a blowfish. Dion used one hand to fan my face. "You're saying that I'm not human? That I'm something *else*?"

"Yeah." Dion's expression melted into concern.

Breathing came easier, but my heart refused to settle down. "And you don't know what that something is?"

He cupped my face, his thumb tracing my cheek. "I wish I did, sweetheart."

And there came the panicked, maniacal breathing again. "I'm going to need something far stronger than a chocolate milkshake to process this, Dion."

"Right. Let me grab our shit to go, and we'll motor to wherever you want." Dion slid from the booth and rested his hands on my shoulders. "Just don't run away on me or anything, yeah?"

"I'm not going anywhere," I whispered, offering him a warm smile.

His shoulders slumped like he'd been tensing. After pressing a quick kiss to my forehead, he whisked over to the bar, grabbed our food, the milkshake, and returned to me with an offered arm. "Where would you like to go, Red? You name it."

The universe only knew what compelled me to give the answer I was about to give. I stood, rubbed the grape cluster charm hanging from the chain around Dion's neck, and whispered, "Your place."

I wasn't sure why I'd expected him to ask me if I was sure, but he didn't. Heat blazed in his eyes, and he wrapped an arm around me, porting us from the diner in front of everyone. We appeared in his apartment, ivy leaves and burgundy star dust cascading around us before disappearing.

"That felt so liberating," I said, not tearing my gaze away from him.

Dion's arm had yet to uncoil from my waist. "Which part?" His voice was gravelly and so incredibly deep.

"That you could openly exhibit your powers without fear of someone seeing. Freedom from *judgment*." My hand moved of its own accord, traveling up Dion's stomach until it reached his lips, my fingers exploring the hair surrounding his mouth.

Dion curled back a corner of his upper lip, making his canines grow ever so slightly. I hovered over one, fascinated by it and curious how much larger they got. "What you thinkin', Red?"

Visions flashed through my mind—Dion crawling over me,

caging me in with those safe, muscular arms, the weight of him as he lowered his hips like pure bliss.

"Devilish, filthy thoughts, Dionysus," I whispered, slipping my finger into his mouth, grinning as he flicked his tongue against it and let one canine graze the skin.

Dion took my hand in his, curling it against his chest. "Even after just learning you're a fairy tale and not knowing which one?"

The question snapped me from some misty haze I'd unknowingly thrown myself into. "I—I don't—"

Grinning, Dion strolled past me, his lips lowering to my ear. "And now you can't blame my godly essence for your desire to have me between your thighs, Chelsea."

My stomach tripped over itself, and I inexplicably forgot how to articulate words. "I never—I mean to say—"

Dion gave a husky chuckle and swatted my ass, making me yelp, heat flooding my neck and face. "How about that drink?"

"Yes, please," I squeaked. Smacking my hands over my face, I turned on a heel, collapsing over the dark marbled bar Dion whisked behind. The dips and grooves of the stonework suddenly became of keen interest. I traced my fingertips across the smoothness, patches of divots and rougher spots tickling my skin. "This is really nice, Dion."

He'd already poured one wine glass and turned with the bottle in his hand, filling the other. An amused smile played on his lips. "Thanks. Here you go. This'll help take the edge off."

"Appreciate it," I responded slowly, taking the fancy goblet with both hands. Pewter grape vines circled the stem, and I busied my thumbs over the design as I took a deep gulp—fruity, earthy, and something I couldn't place. "No offense, but this tastes funny."

Dion let out one of those gravelly chuckles that made me lean in closer to him to feel the vibrations, and I hummed. "None taken. I laced it halfway with ambrosia wine."

I'd begun to sip again, and my brows raised over the rim, my nose in the glass. "Ambrosia?"

"Uh-huh." Dion pressed his forearms to the bar, crossing one over the other. "Not sure you need it yet, given your power hasn't manifested, but figured an extra *kick* wouldn't hurt given the circumstances."

Power. Manifestation. Fucking *magic*. It was all enough to make my head spin, or maybe it was the wine.

Growling, I kicked my heels off and stormed for the living room, where a comfy cream-colored area rug lay, beckoning me to curl my toes on it. "You know what the most frustrating part about all of this is?" I swayed my arms, the glass going with them, sloshing the red contents.

"What's that, Red?" Dion had followed me, and smiling, he gently took the glass from my grasp, filling it with more wine.

"Not knowing what I am or how to figure it out." I raised my hands to the air and let them flop against my thighs in defeat.

"Here." Dion offered me the goblet. I reached for it, but he delicately took my hand and brought the glass to my lips. "You drink, I'll hold. Deal?"

Nodding, a bubbling sensation rising in my belly, I took a sip. "Gods, this stuff works fast, huh?"

"Chelsea," Dion pinched my chin and tilted it upward to look at him. "You *need* to relax."

Relax? What was even the definition of relaxed?

"I guess I don't understand it. My sister was a gift to our family

from the gods turned goddess, that I understand." Opening my mouth to him to indicate I wished for my wine, he obliged, grinning and pouring some past my lips. "But our dad is normal and—" A hollow pit formed in my stomach.

Dion's grip on my hand tightened like he thought I was about to collapse. "Chelsea?"

"Was it my mom? But she never said anything." My breathing grew erratic again, thoughts jumbling, my heart thundering in my chest. "*Why* wouldn't she say anything?" Something sparked in my eyes, the sensation only making the panic worse.

"Chels, Chels, come here," Dion soothed, pulling me to him in an embrace. He wrapped his broad arms around me and held me tight, stroking my hair. "Listen to my breathing. Time it with mine."

Following his words, I pressed my ear to his chest, counting how many times his heart beat for every four or five of my own. Steadily, my breathing returned to normal, and I stood motionless, letting his tightly secured arms make me feel safe.

My mother passed away when my sister and I were children. I was older than Elani when it happened, but I, too, was *so* young and hadn't had a chance to know much about her.

"Want to know what I think?" Dion asked, his voice booming through his chest against my ear.

Not saying anything, I simply nodded.

"I think I should take you home, let you get some rest, and when you wake up, you can take the time to figure it out. Maybe call your sister."

Pushing against him, I peeled back and pouted. "But that means leaving you."

"I'll still be here," Dion said, laughing. "You're not getting rid of me that easily now that you're finally talking to me again, Stewart." He bumped me under the chin with his knuckle.

"But—" I started, the word coming out as one long whine.

Dion trailed a finger down my spine, the contact utterly titillating despite the cloth barrier of my shirt. He rested that same hand on my hip. "We'll have plenty of time for fun later. You figure this out first."

"Fun?" I grinned wickedly. "Is that what you're calling it now?"

"You're right. With me, it's more of a carnal ecstasy." Dion let out a low growl, his nose brushing my cheek, and I could feel the grin on his lips against my skin.

Groaning, I playfully shoved him. "Stop teasing me."

"Come on, Red." Dion cradled me in his arms and ported us to my apartment before I could try to protest.

I'd heard the whooshing of his porting magic, but I rested my head in the crook of his neck and contentedly closed my eyes. His deep, rumbly voice lightly hummed *Lay All Your Love on Me* as he rested me on my bed, but I was already too close to sleep to appreciate it fully.

"Go to sleep, Chelsea." Dion's lips brushed my forehead. "And remember, you need to *relax*."

It was the last thing I heard before my mind and body drifted into slumber, visions of bonfires, dancing shadows, and curved horns overtaking my dreams.

Nine

Chelsea

Groaning, I awoke the next day with the blazing sun piercing my eyeballs through the parted curtains at my front window. I'd typically made every effort to keep them tightly shut to avoid such a natural alarm clock, but Riley wanted to sunbathe. His crème-colored tail with the black tip hung over the couch, occasionally twitching when he saw something that intrigued him outside. My comforter was bunched to my neck, and I yawned, sitting up and groggily trying to recall how I'd gotten here last night.

Apollo. The diner. Dion's place. *Dion.*

Sucking in a quick breath, I peeled back the covers, relieved to see myself in sleep attire—cotton lounge shorts and a lace camisole sans bra. I froze, pressing my thumb between my eyes to think about it more. Riley hopped onto the bed, turning circles until he sat on my lap, staring up at me.

"Magic," I whispered, making Riley perk up, his tiny paws rubbing together. "I'm something magical, Riley."

Riley did several more circles, the most excited I'd seen him since we'd first randomly met in the woods years ago.

Tilting my head, I rubbed a knuckle over Riley's puffed, furry chest. "You weren't lost, were you?"

My ferret took my finger between his paws and rubbed his face against it.

"Oh, gods," I moaned, remembering vividly now that Dion had to carry me home and put me to bed.

That begged the question, did he dress me in my pajamas, or had I? Was it horrible that I'd hoped it *was* him who'd done it?

Dion had held me to him when I went into a panicked spiral, repeatedly telling me to relax. I'd have no hope of figuring out what I was, let alone bringing whatever power I possessed to the surface by clouding my thoughts with fears and worries.

Relax.

Closing my eyes, I envisioned myself packing the boxes before moving to the Cove. What had been stashed away in my closet that I'd forgotten about? There were numerous boxes shoved into corners of high shelves I hadn't seen in years but kept because what was in them held value. Now, where were *those* boxes?

Flashing my eyes open, I was startled at the sight of Riley in the same pose, staring at me as if he were waiting for something. "What's up? Do you need food?" When he didn't budge, I continued to go down the list of essential possibilities. "Water?" The ferret still remained as motionless as a statue. Chuckling, I scooped him into my arm and carried him to the floor with me. "You can help me look through these boxes."

There were only three boxes in my closet, but when I had no idea what I was looking for, the task still seemed so daunting. I could spend hours combing through every photo album, notebook, and memento and still have no idea what I was.

After staring at the boxes like they were an endless, orbiting abyss, I snatched my phone to call my little sister.

A high-pitched yawn was the first thing I heard when she answered on the second ring, "Hello?"

Considering she hadn't said my name meant she didn't look at her phone and that she was probably still half asleep.

"Lani? It's me."

"Oh, Chelsea, hi," Elani responded, perking up, her voice wispier and more attentive.

Chewing my thumbnail, I peered at the boxes and scratched Riley's head. "Did I call you at a bad time? Ugh, you weren't napping, and I woke up the mother of a flying toddler, did I?"

"Chelsea," Elani scolded, raising her voice. "You're my sister. You're allowed to call me whenever you wish, even if you don't know if it'll be inconvenient. I could've not answered the phone and called you back, right?"

I grumbled at how much more mature she sounded over me as of late. "Fine. You're right. How are you?"

"Other than being tired and missing *your* ass, I'm doing okay, I'd say. But the real question is, how are *you*?"

Sighing, I tore the tape from the first box, ready to take a few trips down memory lane with my sister acting as support on the phone. "I know you were younger than I was when mom died, but do you, maybe by some repressed memory, remember anything different about her?"

"Different? You're going to have to be more specific, sis."

Adjusting to sit cross-legged on the floor, I pulled out an old green and yellow blanket my grandmother had made me before Elani was born. It still smelled like lilac and mothballs even after all this time. Thoughts of her crocheting it as I played with wooden blocks pulled a smile to my lips. "I found out something recently— something that won't be shocking to you, but still a bit surprising."

"Are you pregnant? Is it Dion's?"

I let the blanket flop onto the floor and let out an indignant "Lani."

"What?" My sister asked, giggling. "I'm sorry. I'm all ears." She *still* giggled under her breath.

Riley kneaded the blanket and spun a few circles before settling on top of it.

"Remember I told you I moved to Arcane Cove? Do you know much about it?"

Subtle sounds of Hedone's gurgles and coos sounded from the other side as my niece tried to steal Elani's phone. She steadily shushed her child and blew several raspberries on Hedone's cheeks before she wrestled with the phone again. "Sorry, yeah, I've heard of the Cove, but it's mostly been in passing from Apollo and Hermes saying they frequent there. Do you like it?"

Removing a stack of notebooks with random story ideas, doodles, and thoughts, I rested them on my lap and thumbed through them. "I love it, but Dion told me something interesting about it."

More rustling sounded from the other line, followed by a door clicking shut and the tumbler of a lock. "*Dion?* Are you talking to him?"

"Elani, did you just barricade yourself in a room away from your child because you think I have sexy stories to tell you?" As fun as it was to read about a childhood version of myself crushing on the likes of Devon Sawa and Hayden Christensen, these held no clues about my other side.

Elani scoffed. "She's not alone. Eros is out there. And judging by your tone, you *don't* have any scandalous tales?"

"No. But yes, I *am* talking to Dion again. We hung out yesterday, and he informed me that the only beings this place will *allow* into it—have magic in their veins." There was a wooden box with a willow tree carved into the top resting in the crate that I didn't remember having.

Elani went silent for a beat before letting out a light gasp. "Chels, does that mean—wait, then what are you?"

"That's what I'm trying to figure out," I responded, my words trailing off as I picked up the wooden box, rested it on my thighs, and ran my fingers over the design, ridding it of dust that collected in my closet. "Dion thinks it has to do with Mom."

"That's what you meant by different. But if she *was* something other than human, wouldn't she have told *you* at least? Or why hasn't Da mentioned anything?"

Gulping, nerves prickling the back of my neck, I opened the box. "Maybe she kept it a secret."

Riley jumped to his feet and scurried to the now-opened box, his nose twitching through its contents.

"Well, crap, you haven't had signs or anything? No unexplained sparks or inky tendrils floating from your hands?"

Elani's words may have sounded absurd to me weeks ago, but I was also too preoccupied watching Riley sort through the various items in the box. He raised on his haunches with a black velvet pouch held in his teeth.

"Do you have anything of Mom's, Lani?" I asked, holding out my hand to receive the bag from my ferret.

"Only what Da gave me. Her porcelain dish set, a few pieces

of jewelry. Why?"

With shaking hands, I cradled the phone on my shoulder and pulled the drawstring. I'd completely forgotten about the day my mother gave it to me, forgotten I still had it until this very moment. I shook the pendant into my open hand, tears welling in my eyes—a silver chain with four crystals nearing the circular piece, a pentagram overlaying it, at its center a light blue stone, and hanging from the circle were five tear-drop crystals.

"I think I know what mom was, sis. I think I know—what *I* am."

"All of a sudden? Did you find something?"

My sister's words faded into the background as I pulled from a deeply rooted part of my soul, that pivotal memory from my childhood. She'd worn it all the time I knew her, but I never associated it with anything other than being a pretty necklace. That day, she'd removed it from her neck, slipped it into this very bag, and curled my little hand over it. I couldn't recall everything she'd said to me, but one phrase in particular, one she'd spoken in Latin, resonated clear as a bell—*mea parva maga.*

My little witch.

A surge punched at my chest, alerting Riley into a frantic bout of squeaks and circling. Falling back on my elbows, I dropped the phone, faint whispers of snowy white sparkling tendrils fading from my fingertips.

I ran my finger over the pentagram, taking deep, concentrated breaths to keep them from spiraling into chaos.

"Chelsea," Elani's voice shouted from my phone.

Fumbling for it, I pressed it to my ear and smiled. "I'm a witch, Elani."

"A—what?"

Clasping the necklace in my hand, I bit my lower lip, already feeling the magic tickling at the underside of my skin, testing whether I'd let it escape—if I'd *use* it. "I'll talk to you more about it later; I'm sorry, there's just—I need to go somewhere. I love you."

"Wait, Chelsea, seriously? Wh—I love you too."

After ending the call, I clasped the chain around my neck and kissed the top of a very excited Riley's head. Scrambling to my feet, I grabbed a pair of flip-flops, threw on a coat, and clad in a pair of pajamas and determination, I *sprinted* to Dion's place.

With zero regard for Dion's neighbors, I pounded, knocked, and slapped his door with the frantic rhythm of a ravenous rabbit.

"Alright, alright, hold your godsdamned horses," Dion yelled from inside.

My core clenched at the sound of his voice, and I gripped each side of the doorway, impatiently waiting for him to open it.

"You have a lot of nerve—" Dion started but stood still when he saw me. His amber eyes flared to life as he roamed my attire beneath the jacket, which was unabashedly hanging open. "Well, fuck. Hi, Chelsea."

I had no intentions of beating around the bush during my trek over here and had zero plans to change my mind now. "I'm a witch," I breathed out.

Dion arched a brow. "A—"

"A witch, Dion. I'm a *witch*," I repeated, that same white magic sparking and sputtering at my fingertips as if it were trying to figure things out as much as I was.

A devilish grin edged Dion's lips, and he hung one arm on the doorframe above us. "Well, *fuck.*"

An unfamiliar, welcoming fire coiled in my belly, and it was enough to make me throw all caution to the wind, not to think or rationalize and go with precisely what I wanted. *Dionysus.* I leaped, wrapping my arms around his neck and crashing my mouth to his. Dion groaned against my lips. He cradled me with one arm secured under my ass while the other whisked the door shut with a loud, satisfying *bam.*

Still holding me with that same single, sexy arm, he carried me into the kitchen, our mouths devouring the other, tongues dancing like it was the twentieth time we'd kissed versus the first. My fingers tangled in his wavy, raven locks, and when he adjusted his grip, my pelvis pressed tighter against the carved abs I could feel beneath his tank. My budding magic sputtered from my hands, making some of Dion's hair smoke.

Gasping, I peeled away and patted it like embers had formed as if I was that adept with my power yet. "Dion, this just started happening. I have no idea what I'm doing with it or—"

He silenced me with a soft kiss and sat me on the marble kitchen counter, my feet dangling from the edge. Peeling half my jacket over one shoulder, letting his finger graze my skin, he said, "Then lay it all on me, Red. I can handle it."

I curled my legs around his waist and pulled him between my thighs, shrugging the jacket off and away. My hands became tools of frantic, denied desires and greedily clawed at Dion's shirt and pants. A masculine chuckle bubbled from the wine god's throat, and he snatched my wrists, kissing the inside of one palm and then the other.

Grinning, he pressed his hands on each side of my hips, leaning over me until his lips hovered near my ear. "Is my wicked witch *greedy?*"

Hearing him call me that for the first time sent me over the edge, and in answer, I wrapped my hand in his tank top and *tore* it away. I'd half expected the smile on his face to fade when he realized I ruined his shirt, but the grin only broadened, those mischievous canines elongating and pressing ever so slightly into his bottom lip. I let out a shuddering breath at the sight of this man, this *god's* torso. I'd only ever seen his chiseled arms and that wrapping black ivy tattoo on his left shoulder and bicep, but to gaze at his chest and that *stomach*—I wrapped my hands around the back of his neck and pulled his mouth to mine.

Dion returned the kiss, his beard brushing my chin, reddening it. His hands slid up my ribs and under my camisole, and he paused, kissing me only long enough to whisk it over my head. He gripped my hair in one palm while the other dove for my breast, kneading it and tweaking the nipple.

"Lay back," Dion commanded, stepping away to undo his belt, capturing me with his gaze, enticing me to watch him.

Leaning back on my elbows, I chewed on my thumbnail as he slid the pants down, taking the briefs underneath with them to reveal his thickness—hard and ready. My wildest imagination couldn't have conjured any of this. He prowled forward, tracing his hardened palms up my thighs, a low growl emanating from his chest as he ogled his prize. Small claws formed in place of his nails, and I shuddered at the sensation of them scraping my skin without any threat of puncturing. It made me all the more curious about the beastly side of Dion he'd spoken of briefly.

His fingers curled into my shorts, and he slid them down my legs, tossing them aside and immediately spreading my knees apart. Dion's growling intensified as he took me in, staring at what lay between my thighs. He pulled me to the edge of the counter by the backs of my knees and sunk a finger inside me without preamble, and my back arched, a low shrill pushing from my lungs.

"Shit, Red. You're already so wet for me," Dion said, his voice extra husky.

Panting, I reached for his arm, sinking my nails into it once I'd found it. "Dion, I need you inside me right now like I need oxygen to *breathe*."

I wasn't kidding. Whether it'd been my continued denial of what I wanted or this new revelation of my true self and power, the ache in my core was driving me mad.

"Well, then. That's all you had to say," Dion snarled before positioning himself at my entrance and slowly pushing in until our hips met.

"Oh, fucking gods," I cried out, grabbing Dion's shoulders for purchase.

He drove into me like a bear with his mate, and the sensation of it, the ferocity of it, had me unintentionally backpedaling on the counter. Dion wouldn't let me get away, though. He kept tugging me toward him with every thrust. My arms flailed behind me, knocking over several opened, half-full wine bottles, splashing their contents onto the marble, the floor, and my *skin*.

A devious glint formed in Dion's eyes, and he paused, grabbed another bottle, and poured some over my chest. He bent to my breasts, sucking and licking away the wine while continuing to pump in and out of me.

"Open your mouth," Dion beckoned softly and when I did, he poured some of the wine past my lips. I'd recognized the taste from last night—ambrosia wine. The tingling sensation hit my spine instantaneously, and his movements inside me became tenfold. I clenched around him, back arching again.

"Come for me, Chels," he asked, lapping up some more of the wine that collected in the dip between my collarbones.

Dion's filthy words were enough to send me straight to oblivion, and I cried out, my knees pressing against his ribs as I shivered blissfully through my release. My power surged through my veins, releasing from my fingertips and palms as swirly white wisps that made the surrounding lights flicker and the glasses in the cabinets clang together. His hips slowed, moving in languid strokes, his head lowering to my lips, wine dribbling from his mouth into mine. I swallowed it as his tongue dove inside.

Grabbing the tops of my thighs, Dion bucked and thrust harder now, faster, until he stilled, his grip tightening on my legs, those claws puckering against my skin. He let out the sexiest, most satisfied masculine groan as he came undone inside me, giving one final pump before collapsing over me. His forearms caged my head, and he smiled down at me, gaze marveling at the wine stains glistening on my skin.

"I can't say I've ever done anything like that before." I covered my eyes with a hand, biting back an embarrassed smile.

Dion wasn't having it and peeled my fingers away, holding my palm hostage against his. "Done what exactly? Fuck a god as a witch, or be that impulsive?"

"When you put it that way, both, I guess."

Dion snickered and traced infinity symbols through the wine still glazing my stomach. "This is only the beginning, Red."

It hadn't occurred to me in the heat of the moment, but something he'd done made me freeze, and I propped on an elbow, gazing down at him still resting inside me. "That is uh—that isn't going to be a potential problem, is it?"

Dion let his head droop before kissing my clammy forehead. "Oh, Chelsea. I wouldn't have done it otherwise. The Fates have to bless such a thing directly, and they haven't even so much as glanced in my direction since I was a tadpole in my dad's ball sack."

Grimacing at that, I let my finger roam his ivy tattoo. "Was that not a clause that *applied* to your dad? To Zeus?"

"Fate designed his actions. Most of us wouldn't exist, wouldn't be living out our destinies if it weren't for it, but there's a lot to unpack there." Dion pressed a chaste kiss to my lips and slowly pulled out of me, pressing a hand to my lower back to help me sit up. "My family is—complicated."

"Yeah," I whispered, sliding from the counter and rubbing my arms. "Apparently, so is mine." Frowning at the thought, I moved for the expansive windows overlooking Arcane Cove. Most of it consisted of thick forests with towering canopies, but at night, the town's center would blaze with street lamps and neon lighting, and the moon would glow brightly over it all.

"I'm sure she had her reasons for not telling you," Dion said from behind me, his brawny arms like a security blanket wrapping around my waist from behind. "Do you often let a whole town see you naked, or is this something new too?"

Gasping, realizing I was standing in front of a wall of windows without a singular article of clothing on, I went to cover myself with my arms, but Dion held me steadfast. "What? The idea of other people seeing me naked doesn't make you jealous?"

"No," he responded gruffly, his nose grazing my jaw. "Because at the end of the day, *I* am the one inside you."

My core swooped, wetness forming between my thighs again. "Is this going to change things between us, Dion?"

"Yes."

Frowning, I whipped around to face him, searching his expression for an answer to his abruptness. "Why?"

"When, since the dawn of creation, did sex not change something between beings? Between animals, even?" Dion lifted the pentagram pendant on my necklace and held it in his palm for a beat. "You always go straight to the negative. Change isn't always so."

He was right. Discovering my new magical self was helping me figure out my human side as much as the new one.

"Oh, my—Dion, your *floor*," I exclaimed, pointing at the red wine stains on his hardwood floors and white carpet.

"Ain't no thing, sweetheart." Without turning around, Dion snapped his fingers, and the mess was gone as if it never existed. Several filled and corked wine bottles rested on the counter in place of the ones I'd spilled.

Lifting my hand, I snapped my fingers, trying to turn off the lights, or levitate something, or virtually do *anything*. No white magic flowed from my fingertips like it had before, not even pathetic sputters. "I don't understand it. It was glitchy at best, but I can't get it to do it again. How am I supposed to be a witch if I can't even turn off a damn light on command? How do I—" There went the panic again.

Dion yanked me to him and pressed his chest to the side of

my head. "I don't know a lot about witches, but I do know their powers can manifest in times of trauma or intense emotion. In your case, that was the discovery and—" An animalistic snarl vibrated in his chest. "—what we just did in my kitchen."

"It just happened, though. I couldn't do it on purpose if I tried."

Dion grabbed my shoulders and coaxed me back. "Come to the club tonight."

"You mean the one you've owned this entire time and never bothered to tell me?" I folded my arms and raised a brow.

"Don't give me that. I had no idea you were a witch and all walks of magical life come into that place. It would've been *a lot* to take in for you."

"I suppose you're right." I fought the compulsion to roll my eyes and instead cast my gaze to my bare feet, wiggling my toes.

"Come to the club, dress in something saucy, and I guarantee you I'll show you the night of your life, Chels. Maybe it'll spark something."

The thought of dancing with him surrounded by other celestial beings tugged an excited smile to my lips. "Alright. And don't think I haven't forgotten that you still owe me several more client introductions." I pointed a finger in his face.

Playfully, he nipped at it, those sharper canines still pronounced. "There's hardball Stewart. And I'm still good for it." Dion crossed the room, his gorgeous muscular bronzed ass flexing as he picked up my jacket. "I'll port you home."

"Home?" My voice came out as a disappointed squeak.

Dion curled the jacket around my shoulders, rubbing them through the fabric. "Miss me already?"

"Don't flatter yourself," I said, swatting him, but honestly, yes.

"I have to go do mundane club ownership shit, and you should rest with your ferret curled against your side." Dion cupped my chin. "And then we'll have *all* night, Red."

"Riley? Curl up with Riley? He's connected to me somehow, isn't he?"

Nodding, Dion, still very naked, ported us to my apartment. "I forget the term witches use for them, but yeah, I believe he is."

As if on cue, Riley bolted from his carpet tower and scurried figure eights against my ankles.

"I *do* feel exhausted."

Swaggering, Dion's bared cock twitching, he dragged a hand through his hair. "I tend to have that effect."

My cheeks warmed, and I grinned at him, unable to disagree.

Dion let his gaze roam my face and hair before pressing a sensual, toe-curling kiss to my lips. "Satiation looks good on you, Red."

Humming, I lifted to the balls of my feet, not wanting the kiss to end or him to leave, for that matter. I'd become addicted to him and had no explanation for it other than how godsdamned sexy he was and his many—talents. "I'll see you tonight."

"Get some rest," Dion demanded, pointing to my bedroom down the hall. "And take it easy. Your powers *will* come. You have to be patient."

"You say that like you've been around for thousands of years or something." I gave him a sleepy smile, my eyes growing heavy.

Chuckling, he traced a thumb over my lip. "Until tonight, *mágissa.*"

The god of wine and frenzy ported away, leaving only faint wisps of burgundy mist and ivy.

Ten

Dion

What a fucking surprise *that* was. And I'm not the type to be easily taken off guard, but when Chelsea showed up on my doorstep in only a thin tank, her tits visible, and some tiny ass booty shorts? I *am* a god, and I *still* thanked the gods for whatever I had done to deserve such a moment.

"You dog," Hermes said, punching my shoulder.

The club wouldn't open for another couple of hours, and I busied myself with unloading glasses from the dishwasher and setting them up for the club's busiest night of the week. Hermes sat on a stool, Bruce on the one next to him, spinning circles, his hooves raised to the ceiling.

"What?" I grumbled, positioning the glasses in perfect rows, even taking the time to adjust them if they were off.

Bruce paused his circles long enough to scratch one horn and said, "You always regale us with stories of your exploits, and yet with Red?" He made a gesture of zipping his mouth shut.

Hermes pointed at Bruce and interlaced his fingers on the bar top. "What the satyr said."

"Shut up." I reached for another glass, and when I came up with empty air, I grabbed a towel and started wiping anything and everything down. "This is different."

"How so, big guy?" Hermes blinked his blue eyes at me, feigning ignorance.

There was an exceptionally stubborn grease mark, and I growled, rubbing at it furiously. "Shit, I don't know. I feel—protective over her."

Bruce scooted forward on his seat. "Like a mate?"

"No," I frowned, the idea of that *not* being true irritating me. "I mean, maybe? Fuck if I know."

Hermes scoffed and raked a hand through his brown locks. "Wow. This is really getting to you, huh?"

"Look, you two." Throwing the towel down with extra fervor, making them both zip to attention, I pressed my palms to the bar. "I feel something different toward Chelsea than I have with anyone else. And if she *was* my mate, how would I be able to tell?"

Bruce burst out laughing, resting his hands on his portly stomach. "You'd know. Trust me."

"Not necessarily," Hermes countered, fluttering his fingers at Bruce.

"Yeah." I playfully punched Bruce in the shoulder, making him wobble on his stool. "Like you have experience."

"Now, I never said that. I only know because I talk to a lot of people. One tends to hear things." Bruce got momentarily distracted by a maenad strolling past, setting up tables. He licked two fingers, ran them up the length of his horns, and made a motion like he was about to abandon the conversation, but I grabbed his vest and stopped him.

"You said not necessarily, Herm. What did you mean by that?" Keeping Bruce still until he relented, I nudged my chin at Hermes.

"A lot of us have found mates, but there's not one all-encompassing type amidst so many varieties of celestial beings. You have fated mates—" Hermes lifted a finger for each phrase. "—fated bonds, soul mates, and Tartarus, I don't know what shifters call it, but their *mating* is an entirely different game."

I stroked my beard, mulling over Hermes' words. What if Chelsea and I were mates in the shifter sense? I did, after all, have the capability to shift into a more beast-like form. "That still doesn't answer my question on how we would know."

"What is she, anyway?" Bruce asked, snatching a cocktail straw to gnaw on like a goat.

"A witch," I responded, my dick getting hard at the memory of the brightened look on her face when she'd told me. It was like the revelation breathed new life into her.

Hermes stood on the rung of his stool and shoved my shoulder, a wide-ass grin on his face. "Well, hot damn, bro. Has she shown any powers yet?"

Grabbing the towel again, I wiped down the liquor bottles. "Not really. Only some bright white tendrils when she ca—" I stopped and glared at them. "Not really."

"You should take her to talk to the Crone," Bruce suggested, nodding his head as if he had all the witchy answers.

Hermes slapped a hand over his face. "I highly doubt she prefers to be called that, Bruce."

"Why wouldn't she? That *is* what she is. Because she certainly ain't no Maiden or Mother." Bruce gave an exaggerated shrug before waving us off and moving the straw to the other side of his mouth.

Hermes sighed. "He's referring to the High Priestess, Cressida, Dion. And despite the satyr's insane disregard for manners, it's not a bad idea."

It wasn't as if I hadn't thought about it. Everyone in the Cove knew who to go to with any questions or concerns involving witches.

"I will, but Chelsea wants to come into her own, and I don't blame her. I think it's best if she discovers her powers first, whatever that might be." Throwing the towel at Hermes' chest, annoyed when he snatched it from mid-air with lightning speed, I added, "That's why I invited her here tonight. To get her to unwind. She's so high-strung it stresses *me* out at times. It's gotta be holding her back."

Bruce showed us his ass, making his bushy satyr tail sway. "Get her to unwind. Rail her in the backroom. We know where you're going with this."

I grabbed the towel and hurled it at Bruce, making it land on his horns and covering his face.

"What you *should* do is take her to the VIP room," Hermes suggested with a wicked smile, nudging his head at the black door with gold lettering labeled VIP Only.

The VIP area at Bacchus wasn't like your typical champagne room with lounging, ordering liquor by the bottle, and private dancers. Here, it led to my ancient sanctuary in the forest where the real festivities took place—dancing around a bonfire, usually naked, potential orgies, music from wind instruments, and drinking. Lots and lots of drinking.

Blowing out a breath, I grabbed the bar top's edge. "I'm not sure if she's ready for that."

Fucking Olympus, how I wished she was, though. To witness her in complete abandon, to make her feel like the flaming seductress she was—I adjusted my pants and cleared my throat.

"By Valhalla, is that you, Dion?" An all-too-familiar baritone voice boomed from the other side of the mostly vacant space.

He strolled closer, his tall, wide form hovering above mine by several inches, which always irritated the Tartarus out of me. Half of his long, red hair was pulled into a bun at the center of his skull, and his fiery orange eyes landed on me with a brightened smile.

"Thor. Fancy seeing you here. It's been, what? A hundred damn years?" Smirking, I offered him a forearm that he shook.

"At least. But believe it or not, I got bored on Asgard and thought I'd see why you Greeks preferred a life of disguise over rubbing elbows and drinking wine in the clouds of Olympus." Thor combed a hand through his long beard and surveyed the club.

Hermes turned in his stool, seemingly unimpressed by the Norse god, and leaned back on his elbows. "Don't you have giants to fight off?"

"Not sure we've met." Thor offered his forearm to Hermes.

Hermes narrowed his eyes at the god of thunder as if sizing him up while locking arms with him. "Hermes."

"Ah, yes. You're the one that can run really, really fast, right?" Thor pantomimed quick legs in the air with two fingers and let out a hearty chuckle.

Laughing for only a moment, I clapped Hermes on the back. "He's also the only god any of the others trust with important messages. 'Ol Herm here has saved my ass a time or two, I'll tell ya that much."

Hermes elbowed me in the ribs, and grinning, shook his head. "Don't get soft on me, Dion, just because you've finally got a crush on a female."

"Oh?" Thor propped against one of several ionic columns that bordered the dance floor. He folded his arms, making the black shirt he wore tighten on his biceps, and I fought the urge to roll my eyes.

Bruce's hooves clacked on the tile floor as he walked to Thor. "Pardon me, good sir, but might I trouble you to see your hammer?"

Thor glanced down at the satyr before turning his gaze to me, silently confirming if my friend was serious. I shrugged. "You would need one of my iron gloves to hold Mjölnir, satyr, and I don't think they'd uh—" He eyed Bruce's petite hands. "—fit."

"Pfft," Bruce guffawed, flicking one horn. "I don't need no fancy gloves."

"Suit yourself," Thor replied, snapping his fingers and making the golden hammer with Nordic scrolling carved into the metal appear, its hilt a thin, short wooden rod wrapped in leather binding. It made a wall-shattering *boom* when it landed just shy of Bruce's hooves.

Bruce rubbed his hands together and lifted, only managing to move it an inch, but it didn't stop him from repeatedly trying. We'd be hearing cursing, grunts, and growls from him for the next several minutes.

"Why'd you come to the Cove, Thor? Why not Midgard, as you call it?" I asked, popping open the cash register to ensure there was adequate change.

All forms of gods may have had different terminology for it, but a place for humanity always existed no matter how they spun the stories.

"I've been to Midgard plenty of times, but somehow, this place slipped through my celestial fingers. And when I saw the name Bacchus, well, it didn't take the wisdom of Frigg to figure out who owned this place." Letting out a deep chuckle, Thor displayed his hands at the surrounding club, swiveling his hips.

"Yeah? What do you think of it?" Smirking, I tapped the touchscreen credit card device, ensuring it was in working order.

"It's very you, Dion. Very you," Thor replied, eyeing Bruce still fiddling with his hammer.

Bruce licked his hands, slapped them together, and did several quick exhales. He squatted on his haunches and attempted to lift with his legs, falling backward when the hammer won yet another battle.

"And don't think you're getting out of this female business, the Speedster briefly brought up," Thor added, pointing at me.

Hermes flashed me a devious grin as he faced the bar again. "Yeah. Thinks she might be his *mate*."

"For the umpteenth time, Herm, if she were, you'd think the Fates would've given me some kind of sign." A snarl wrapped my words in a tightly annoyed package.

Thor patted Bruce's head before pressing a finger to his hammer, making it disappear in a swirl of embers and orange sparks. Bruce's shoulders slumped. "I'm not entirely sure if your Fates work like our Norns, but their 'signs,' as you called them, can be about as subtle as a sudden chilled breeze on a hot summer's day."

Hermes stuck his bottom lip out, contemplating this. "That sounds about right for our conniving thread weavers as well."

"You do all realize your help is about as useful as spectacles for a cyclops, right?" I blinked at them, irritation wringing my spine like a drenched sponge.

Music began to blare from the overhead speakers, the multi-color lights spilling over the bar and dancefloor. Maenads circled through the scattered tables, resting newly filled napkin dispensers and Bacchus coasters on each. The night's bartenders, a male demon with dark blue stubbed horns and a light pink pixie with her translucent wings flapping through her white shirt, joined me behind the bar, surprise at my presence evident on their faces.

"You said she's coming tonight, right, boss?" Bruce asked, rubbing his biceps from the strain of attempting to pick up the hammer.

"Yeah," I replied, my voice distant. My gaze was glued to the entrance as patrons began flooding into the club, all smiles and excitement to get their night of debauchery started. A peculiar bout of nerves fluttered through my stomach, making my chest tighten. As each person entered, the nerves multiplied when I'd yet to spot *her*.

Thor cracked his knuckles, spotting something he liked across the room, but I was too fixated on the entrance to glance away. He jostled me. "I'll meet up with you later, Dion. Going to make the most of my night here in the Cove."

"Have fun," I mumbled.

The planet somehow slowed on its axis, the pounding bass of the music timing with my ethereal heartbeat as I lay eyes on Chelsea entering *my* club. She wore a gold, sequined dress that cut off at mid-thigh. The front had a plunging neckline that went just above her belly button, giving a prime view of those ample tits I had in my mouth and hands the night before. Her hair was fiery and voluminous in tight waves over her shoulders. To my relief, she was alone and her gaze flitted around her, searching for me. She turned away, revealing an entirely backless dress stopping above her ass and showing those two dimples there. When she spun around, our gazes instantly locked through the crowd. A surge I'd never experienced sparked in my tailbone, zipped up my spine and cemented itself in my skull. There was no denying it now.

Chelsea Stewart was my mate. She was *mine*.

Eleven

Chelsea

I'd stood outside the club pacing a square on the sidewalk with my clutch tucked under my arm for the better part of ten minutes after they officially opened. Was I absurd for pursuing this? Granted, I'd already dug myself pretty damn deep by jumping Dion's bones this morning. What was to say it wouldn't be more than a fling? Would that be a bad thing? Did he want more? Did I want more?

My power sizzled in my palm and zapped my middle finger. Yelping, I shook my hand and stared at my skin. Was that some form of magical defense mechanism when I got in my own head? Growling in frustration, I marched to the line now wrapped around the building and waited. Dion said Bacchus attracted all walks of ethereal life, but no one seemed out of the ordinary at first glance. That was, of course, if you ignored the variety of insect-like, feathered, and taloned wings sprouting from guests in the queue.

When I reached the bouncer, I fumbled with my clutch, ready to produce my ID, but he waved me in, grumbling and motioning

91

for those behind me to move forward. One step over the threshold from outside the blazing, booming atmosphere of the club had my arm hairs standing on end. I was no stranger to the club scene, but it had been years since I set foot in one and never a place like this. Bacchus was like stepping into something from a storybook, with rows of marble columns lining both floors and sputters of glowing, glittering magic from dancing patrons at every corner.

Scanning the main floor, I saw no signs of Dion and felt compelled to pull the hem of the sultry dress I'd brazenly chosen. It didn't budge more than half an inch, but the chilled breeze wafting against my exposed chest and back from overhead industrial-sized vents made me acutely aware of how scandalous my attire was. I'd be lying to myself if I said I decided on it because I wanted people to stare because I wanted *his* eyes on me—I wanted to have him spellbound.

A hulking form passing jolted me from my daydream. He was easily several feet taller than me, with veined bat-like wings the height of his body. His haunches were clawed, hooved, and massive, matching his equally large hands with three wide fingers, talons curling from each. He'd paused to look down at me, dipping his squared chin, the corners coming to jagged points, and when he offered a half-smile, similar sharpened canines to Dion's glinted from the strobe lights.

"Beg your pardon," he said, his voice deeper than the Titans trapped underground, and I fought the urge to stare at the massive, curved, swirling horns protruding from his forehead. He wore a leather kilt and a simple vest over his bulbous arms and chest.

"Um, hello?" A male voice said from the opposite side of the room, the tone lighter than the average. "I thought gargoyles were supposed to be protective? Care to do your job, you big oaf?" The man, dressed in stark white pants, loafers, and a bright red shirt exposing his chest and golden chains, nudged several of the people surrounding him, who were all cackling.

Grumbling, the gargoyle moved past me and to the awaiting male, his forked tail swaying behind him. "I've got to find new clients."

When the gargoyle was no longer blocking my view, I zeroed in on Dion's piercing gaze instantaneously despite the dozens of bodies between us. Something happened in that moment I couldn't explain, but my magic sputtered at my fingertips, a tingle trickling down my spine until it landed in my tailbone, intensifying there. I'd suddenly developed the overwhelming urge to get to him, and, keeping my eyes locked with his, I pushed through the horde, irritation bubbling with each passing second that I wasn't *with* him.

The one instant I blinked, I'd lost sight of him, and the pulsating music fell from my ears, my quickened breaths replacing it. I spun circles, confused and erratic, the rotating lights and shoulders bumping into me from every angle, doing nothing to soothe me.

"Hey, Red," Dion's voice, like liquid chocolate, rumbled in my ear from behind me. His arm snaked around my waist, his palm resting on my stomach, and I *melted* against him.

Threading my fingers with his, I finally found the will to open my eyes after letting his scent tantalize my senses. "This place is amazing."

A brief chuckle thundered from his chest, his lips feathering my ear lobe before he playfully nipped at it. "The night hasn't even started, Stewart."

Dion had many nicknames for me, but I'd come to learn whenever he referred to me with my last name, he intended to challenge me.

Challenge accepted, frenzy god.

Turning, I held the metallic gold clutch in one hand and hung my fingers from his belt loop with the other. "I'm all yours. What do you want to do with me?"

Dion's gaze shot downward to my hand hovering near his crotch, and he frustratedly dragged a hand over his beard. "Gods and martyrs, Chels. What *am* I going to do with you?"

The question had my heart racing, core clenching, and my magic humming in my veins.

Dion pulled me to him, my breasts thumping against his ribs and making me gasp. "For starters—" He plucked the clutch from my vice-like grip and held it up between us. "You're not going to need this."

That calm demeanor I pretended to exude moments prior? Gone and scorched.

"But my—"

Dion cut my words short by slipping his hand to my exposed lower back, his forefinger resting on one of two dimples there as if he'd already perfectly mapped my body. "Tambie, would you be a dear and lock this in the safe?" He said to a female with small antlers extending from her forehead and a pixie haircut carrying a silver tray. Dion dropped my clutch onto it.

"You got it, boss," Tambie answered, flashing me a sultry grin and unabashedly roaming my body with her gaze.

I turned to follow her, but Dion's grip tightened on my back. "Dion, my credit cards are in there, my ID, my—"

"*Mágissa*," Dion whispered, beckoning me to settle on his gaze. He rested a knuckle under my chin and tilted it upward. "Do you trust me?"

Yes, and no? My gut told me I could trust him, but the rational part of my brain questioned how that was possible given the short time I'd known him.

"Yes?" I'd dragged out the word, squinting one eye.

Grinning, Dion kissed me delicately, slipping my upper lip between his. "By the end of the night, I hope to turn that question into a definitive answer."

My eyes remained closed as I waited for the kiss to continue, but I blinked when his hand wrapped with mine.

"But first, you need a little *encouragement*," Dion said, lightly tugging me toward the bar.

Letting him pull me, giggling over it, I leaned an elbow on the bar once we'd reached it. "Ambrosia wine? Is that your plan? Get me intoxicated and throw all scruples to the wind?"

Dion became transfixed on the dip at the front of my dress, his finger lazily tracing circles on exposed skin above the fabric. "Part of it. Encouraging beings to let loose and have fun happens to be my specialty, but you, my dear Chelsea—" The bartender handed him two drinks, and Dion offered me one. "—have been an enigma."

The idea of my making things difficult for him gave me a perverse thrill.

Taking the drink, I raised it to him. "Here's to challenges then."

"To cracking your nut, Stewart," Dion countered, a delicious twinkle casting in his eyes as he tapped his glass against mine.

A massive golden statue toward the back captured my attention—a man with long, wavy hair and a full beard lounging on a bench in only a toga that exposed his chest, stomach, and legs. One hand raised a goblet, a pitcher hanging lazily by one finger in the other, and clusters of grapes and pine cones were strewn on his lap and at his feet.

"Dion, is that monstrous statue supposed to be you?" I'd paused mid-drink to gawk at it and still held my glass near my lips.

Dion shifted his glance behind him, barely looking at the statue before turning back to me. "I happen to think it's one of the best likenesses anyone has sculpted of me."

Laughing, I pointed at it with my glass. "I'm not denying that, but did it have to be so—" Searching for a word that wouldn't come out naughty proved impossible. "—egotistically huge?"

"I don't know," Dion whispered, leaning in closer. "You've experienced it. Do you think the ego is warranted?"

We grinned at each other over the rims of our cups, and I licked my lips of excess sweet yet earthy alcohol. "This tastes different than before."

"That's because it is." Dion curled his fingers over my hips, urging me closer and propping one of his feet on a stool rung, pressing that thigh against me. "Why are you so high-strung, anyway? You've got a great career; you're hot as Olympus forges and have a great family. Why so stressed?"

Taking several more gulps of my drink, I rubbed the pentagram pendant between two fingers. "Wow, going straight for the jugular that fast, huh?"

Chuckling, Dion dragged a knuckle from one corner of my jaw to the other. "I have to act fast. Get the serious stuff out of the way. Because after two more of those, I'm going to have to fight anyone who tries to touch you when you insist on dancing with the maenads." Dion jutted his chin at the group of females dancing between columns with petite antlers like Tambie had.

Cackling, I swatted his shoulder. "Please. That doesn't sound like me at all."

"I doubt that. Somewhere in there is a woman who wants nothing more than to drop everything, let her shoulders relax, and do whatever the fuck comes to mind without judgment or consequence." Dion tilted his head, studying me. "Tell me. What made you this way?"

Despite everyone dancing around us, the loud music, and flashes of rainbow lighting, I couldn't help but focus on him. Sighing, I downed the rest of my drink and slammed the glass on the bar top. Dion lifted a finger toward it, swirling burgundy magic, and a breath later, more wine filled my glass.

"I'm not blaming my mom or my sister, but her passing away as young as we were and how *very* young Elani was, I pretty much became a parent way too early."

Dion kept his gaze on me, sipped his drink, and let it dangle between two fingers. "What about your dad?"

My eyes widened at Dion implying my dad didn't do his job. "Oh, no, no. My dad was amazing. He suddenly got stuck single-parenting two young girls and did the best he could. But he also had to work a lot to support us, which left us alone and me in charge." Shrugging, I guzzled more of my wine. "It was just the way the cookie crumbled."

Dion nodded thoughtfully and pulled me even closer until we breathed the same air. "And now you feel any moment you crack would be equivalent to letting people down around you. Am I close?"

Dionysus was the first person to ever say those words to me—

words I knew were valid but could never come to grips with myself.

Breathlessly, I nodded at him, and he cupped my chin, kissing me. "Finish that and dance with me." Dion gestured at my glass.

Dion had already been halfway to standing by the time I swallowed the last gulp. He gently took the goblet from my hand and rested it on the bar before leading me to the dancefloor. The patrons seemed to part for him, the owner, the boss, the fucking frenzy god in their midst. The ambrosia wine had my mind slightly hazy, but I was still aware and attentive to everything happening, which made my relaxed state that much more exhilarating.

Dion's arm wrapped around me, his hand delving into my dress to rest on my ribs. I moved closer to him, pressing my hips against his, and as the next song boomed over the speakers, I flashed a brilliant smile. *Lay All Your Love on Me*, but a techno version with thundering bass.

"Is this your doing?" I asked, snaking one hand to rest on the back of his head.

Dion kissed and sucked my neck before grazing his lips at my ear. "It's magic, *mágissa*. Why don't you try to listen to yours? There's so much of it from others in here, you could siphon it from them—from *me*."

Static beaded my skin, my power humming in my veins, agreeing with the Greek god's suggestion. Our bodies swayed in unison, hips flush against one another, and his cock hardening and thickening underneath his pants had my heart racing. Dion was right. The magic here, circling together from dozens of people, letting it freely roam in the atmosphere, made my own feel cataclysmic, urging me to let *go*. Every time I thought it was about to breach the surface, however, I hesitated, fearing what it'd do, and swallowed it back.

"Sweetheart," Dion growled, his lips trailing my exposed shoulder and up my neck again, his hand moving to the front dip of my dress, sneaking his fingers to one breast. "*Relax.*"

Moaning at the sensation of his rough fingers tweaking my nipple, I dug my nails into the back of his head. No sooner had I succumbed to the pleasure than my magic swirled from my palms, forming a glittering snowy white halo around Dion. It settled on him, focused on him, and wouldn't relent—like it was trying to tell me something. I flashed my eyes open, spying Dion's gaze roaming my magic hovering over him. Every compulsion in me wanted to apologize for it, to ensure that it was okay, but I stopped myself. He rewarded me with a sultry grin.

"Your magic seems to have a fascination with me," Dion whispered.

Standing on the balls of my feet, I sucked Dion's earlobe into my mouth, nibbling, no, *biting* it. He let out a gratified snarl. "*I'm fascinated with you, Dionysus. I'm fucking obsessed with you.*"

Tendrils of his burgundy powers intertwined with my ivory magic, the two mingling together as if this was the way it was meant to be. The combined magic spiraled around us from our feet to our heads, and Dion's eyes darkened, his hand grazing my outer thigh before skirting to the inside and up. When he reached my bare folds, I gasped and grinned at him discovering my little secret.

"Fuck," Dion said gruffly, slipping a finger inside and relishing the way I reacted—my head tilted back, breaths turning into pants, as I dug my nails into his shoulders.

"Dion," I moaned, my magic pulsing around him now, pulling him closer until our bodies were pressing so hard our heartbeats became one.

Dion chuckled and nuzzled my chin with his nose, that devilish finger still moving and curling inside me. "I can't get any closer, Chels."

"Let's sneak into a dark corner somewhere. Between this and my magic, I—"

Dion cut off my words by engulfing my mouth with his, kissing me with such depth it made me see stars behind my eyelids. When he pulled away, his finger slipped out, and he adjusted my dress with one tug. "Come with me."

Dion took my hand in his, leading us past dozens of swaying bodies either simulating sex or discreetly having it right there on the dancefloor. Dion made a circular gesture above his head and the females he'd referred to as maenads began to follow us, dropping their trays or stopping their dancing to let the male demons take over. He didn't stop until we stood in front of a charcoal door with crimson-red borders and a velvet rope hanging across it.

Dion slipped a hand to my ass and pulled me to his side, shoving the rope away and using his burgundy magic to unlock the door. Just as white moonlight spilled from the door's crevice as it opened, I caught sight of the metallic sign on the front.

The VIP Room: By Invitation *Only*.

Twelve

Chelsea

I'd expected to walk into a room, per the label on the door, but what I stepped through was a portal to another *realm*. It wasn't a lounge area with plush seating or a rounded table in the center for a dancer. Forests of thick canopies extended as far as the eyes could see, a bonfire roaring in the central cleared space on the dirt. The flames were so expansive I could feel its heat on my face from afar, and I pressed a hand to my cheek.

"Dion," I whispered, my voice wispy and ethereal. "What is this place?"

Dion took my hand, leading me closer to the fire and rubbing between my knuckles. "My sanctuary."

The maenads sprinted past us, their arms raised to the starlit skies, whooping and screeching with joy. Two of them began removing articles of clothing, leaving them in a wayward trail behind them. I tensed at the sight.

Dion gently pulled me to him. "Nothing will happen here that you don't want, Chelsea. But know, this is your opportune moment to be completely unbridled. No judgment. No consequence."

The notion struck a surge from my toes to my core, and when the music played from the branches above, I squeezed Dion's fingers. Biting back a smile, I kicked off my heels and followed the maenads to the fire, joining in a tribal woodland dance and circling it. The flickering flames made my vision hazy when I peered through them, spotting the maenad he'd called Tambie staring at me from the opposite side. Dion leaned against a tree, watching me with a glowing amber gaze. Between Dion's lustful eyes following my curves and Tambie's seducing glances, I found myself fully letting go.

My hands trailed up and over my breasts, some of the dress peeling back and exposing a nipple that puckered once the heat from the fire mixed with the cool forest breeze hit it. I spun circles in the dirt, letting it cake between my toes, my fingers raking through my hair, and I moaned from the unfamiliar freedom settling over me in delicious waves.

"Let it out," a female voice whispered.

"Complete abandon," said another.

My magic pooled in my belly, pulsating and thrashing. The way my body moved delved into something far more feral than the swirling arms and swaying hips it started as. The magic in my veins sizzled up my arms now, striking every neuron on its trek to my head. When it reached my mind, something snapped inside me. Visions of three women dressed in flowing white robes dancing around a similar fire and repeating a chant in a language I couldn't understand flashed before me.

A delicate hand, not Dion's, cascaded over my cheek, enticing me to open my eyes. A maenad offered me a sparkling grin, continuing to dance. "No judgment, Chelsea."

Rough fingers trailed up my back, settling on my dress's clasp. I'd recognize that touch anywhere—Dionysus' touch. With one precise flick, he'd undone the clasp, and the top part of my dress fell to my hips, exposing my breasts. Dion kissed first my shoulder, then my neck. "How do you feel?"

Moaning, I let my head fall back, expecting it to land on his shoulder, but it met with abandoned air. Gasping, I turned to find him, but Dion had become a chuckling shadow, mixing with the other mirages created by the moon and fluttering flames.

A feathered touch grazed the side of my left breast, and I shivered.

"No consequence," Tambie, the maenad from earlier, said, standing in front of me now. She leaned forward, pressing a light kiss to my lips like a calming breeze.

My eyes fell shut again, several feminine hands dragging through my hair, tracing my shoulders and down my arms. My magic swirled around my body and in between my legs like infinity. Two maenads took my hands, one in each of theirs, leading me somewhere. Another tugged the dress down my legs from behind me, and like a choreographed routine, I stepped out of it.

Lazily, I opened my eyes in time to scan the mossy seat they were guiding me toward. It was fit for woodland royalty. Dionysus' throne, perhaps?

Dion's scent filled the air, and I knew he was behind me before he'd outstretched his hand. Turning to face him, I splayed my fingers toward his head, encouraging my magic to dance around him. It paid particular attention to the top portion of his skull, and I suddenly became curious about what his beast looked like. Would he show me it here?

A deep, guttural growl fluttered from Dion's chest, and he

grabbed my ass, pulling me flush against him. "The witch desires to meet my beast, does she?"

Licking my lips, thirsty for it, for him, I faintly nodded.

Lightly, Dion gripped my face and methodically shook his head—left to right. "Say it, *mágissa*."

Puffing my chest, I let my fingers play in his maroon magic floating from his skin, anticipating my answer. "Show me your beast, Dionysus."

A feral grin tugged at the corner of Dion's lips, those deadly canines already growing. His hand loosened on mine as the maenads guided me backward, and I held onto him until only our fingertips brushed and my palm remained outstretched. Dion didn't move, standing still until the maenads lowered me to the mossy throne, encouraging me to settle into whatever was about to happen.

Following their instruction, I sat with my arms resting on the elongated, risen stones on each side of my hips. Instinctively, I drew my knees up, keeping them closed, and gulped at Dion's burgundy magic building around him, growing denser and smokier than I'd seen it before. The maenads combed their fingers through my hair, Tambie using her claws to scrape against my scalp from behind me. Another female's claws traced circles on my shoulders.

Dion displayed his arms at his sides, the smoke billowing at his feet, his transformation starting there—clawed haunches replaced toes and ankles, his legs became wider with bulging veins, and bulking with ethereal muscle. His length remained almost the same save for a bulbous portion that now formed at the top of his shaft. His chest and arms doubled in size, the hair growing denser and more wolfish. The claws I'd gotten a glimpse of earlier were larger and slightly more curved. Dion's head fell back, a low roar emanating from his stomach, growing louder and more intense as the magic worked around his chin, settling on his forehead. When he lifted his skull, he peered at me with radiantly glowing amber eyes and two blackened, ribbed, curved horns extended from his temples, tucking against his head.

My magic burst from my skin, darting straight for the frenzy god, curling his arms and tugging him toward me. I sat up on my elbows, the maenads encouraging me with gentle strokes, using their hands to keep me still. Wetness formed between my thighs, my core throbbing, and stomach tightening. Dion chuckled and smiled with those full wolfish canines, the teeth behind them sharper now, too. He let my magic lead him to me, his arms extended in front of him, at my mercy.

When he reached the moss, I called my ivory magic back to me and bit my lip as Dion walked his fingers up my calf, resting his hand on my knee. "She *likes* the beast." He slipped his hands between my knees and yanked them apart, gaze falling to the wetness *leaking* from me now because of him. "I knew there was a vixen in there somewhere, Chels."

His calling me Chels grounded me for a moment, his way of a reminder that despite what I saw in front of me, he was still the same Dion. His hands curled around my thighs, and he tugged me downward until my ass rested on the seat's edge.

"My maenads are going to cherish you, *mágissa* and I—" Dion sank to his knees, using the back of one claw to lightly graze my soaked folds. "—intend to *worship* you."

Excited breaths escaped me, and my mouth fell open. Tambie

lowered her lips to mine and kissed me, soothing my nerves, her hand finding one of my breasts, kneading it, and pinching a nipple between two claws. She pulled away, her other hand moving to the back of my head and lifting it, giving me a better view of Dion's face sinking between my legs.

"You better hold on," Dion said, his tone deep, gravelly, and feral.

Another maenad guided my hand to one of Dion's horns. She grinned at me once my fingers wrapped around it. Dion let his tongue slip from his mouth, its length longer than that of a human's, and his eyes flashed before he lapped me from my opening to my clit, up and down several times, groaning against my folds as he did it.

My back arched from the moss. "Gods. Oh, *gods*," I cried out.

Four maenads surrounded me, their hands exploring my breasts, my hair, and stomach. Their tongues found my mouth and nipples, licking, sucking, and nipping. Tambie paid especially close attention to me, her kisses the most profound, deeper, and more sensual. I'd never kissed a woman—her lips far softer, tender, and ravenous than I could've imagined.

Dion moved to my clit, the tip of his tongue flicking and circling until his mouth covered it, and he *sucked*. My hips bucked, and I grabbed hold of both horns now, my grip tightening so harshly it turned my knuckles white. When I could feel his satisfied smile against my folds as he continued to tantalize me with his wicked tongue, I used his horns to pull him tighter against me.

Dion pushed my thighs open and wider before propping my ass up. When his tongue disappeared from my seam, I almost whimpered in its absence. He kissed the inside of one thigh, then the other, his canines dragging over the sensitive flesh, pushing against it just enough to make me cry out, but they didn't puncture. Without warning, his tongue plunged inside me, reaching all the way to that sensitive spot inside, flicking against it.

I couldn't help the writhing, pleasurable mess my limbs had become, and the maenads gently kept me put, still caressing and kissing my skin from my stomach to my forehead. Dion's grip tightened around my thighs, refusing to let me scurry away as he continued to fuck me with his beast's tongue. The euphoria built, twisted, and erupted, allowing me my release. My magic poured from my hands, scattering around the maenads, giving them thankful shimmers of ecstasy.

When Dion pulled away, his beard glistening from my arousal, I sat up, panting, my skin flushed pink. Desire awakened for something else entirely, surging in waves from my pores.

Dion dragged a finger over his lips, gathering some of my juices on his finger before slipping it into his mouth. "Leave us," he growled.

The maenads, still coming down from the pleasure my magic had brought them, frowned and whined. Their naked forms stood and took tentative steps away from us, obeying the wine god.

"Don't worry, my precious maenads." Dion locked his carnal gaze with mine, enticing me to gulp. He crawled over top of me, his now massive hands grasping my hips. "You can *watch*."

And with a claiming stare that belonged solely to his beast, he flipped me to my knees and propped my ass in the *air*.

Thirteen

No being in existence had ever thrown my mind off its fucking axis the way Chelsea Stewart has done. Her desire, her willful participation, and the smoldering stare she gave my beast as it appeared inch by inch. Most females only ever requested the horns once they'd seen me in full form, fearing the rest of me or finding it disdainful. Not Chelsea. If anything, her lust deepened, and pure hellfire flashed in her wanting gaze. Not once did she shy away from the maenads' attention either, which only made my heart race faster.

As much as I wanted to keep my face buried in that sweet nectar collecting in her pussy, the pulsing need to be inside her was bordering on pain. The beast would have none of it. It used to be an unruly creature in my youth, wreaking havoc and chaos in its path. I hadn't always possessed the ability either—a side effect from a powerful jealous goddess wishing to see me dead and *almost* succeeding. A wolf shifter friend helped me control it, and I have used it many times through the centuries as a means of intimidation, very rarely unleashing it for sweaty rolls in the sheets. But for Chelsea? My sexy, confident, powerful Chelsea, I'd transform into it whenever she damn well pleased.

Her ass was poised in the air, and Chelsea bent lower until her elbows rested on the moss of my forest throne. She peered at me over her shoulder, those emerald eyes going hooded, crimson flushing her cheeks from my tongue making her come.

Chelsea grabbed her ass cheeks and pulled them away from each other, revealing more of that pretty pink pussy she offered me. "What are you waiting for, Dion? Or are you going to make me beg for it?"

It was tempting, but not this time. The beast was all too consuming, lashing at my skull, and the blood rushing to my dick made it twitch several times, the tip already beading with pre-cum. With a snarl, I grabbed her hips and drove into her, knowing from the glistening wetness coating her slit and trickling down the insides of her thighs she was already more than ready for me. A sultry gasp followed by a moan fluttered from her porcelain throat, and she dug her nails into the stone.

Keeping hold of her waist with one hand, I moved the other to her shoulder, using it to drive her back onto me harder and faster. The growls pushing from my gut were the sounds that only my beast could make, and knowing what Chelsea could mean to us, *for* us, fueled the raging fire, igniting it into an inferno. This witch, this woman, could very well be my mate, and even if she wasn't, I wanted to make her mine.

Chelsea threw her head back, slamming her ass against my stomach and pushing more of me inside her. "Fucking hell, Dion," she groaned, a thin sheen of sweat forming down her spine.

Her ivory magic floated from her skin, giving her a shimmering silhouette. It coiled her stomach and legs until it wrapped around my hips, encouraging me to take her, to conquer her. Leaning forward and still thrusting, I reached between Chelsea's legs, using a knuckle to rub her clit. I trailed my tongue over the sweat collecting on her skin until I reached her shoulder, licking, kissing, and grazing my canines over her there.

It would be so quick. One bite. One blissful moment to sink my teeth into her, to mark her as mine. But I couldn't. Despite the beast's disapproving tugs at my mind, I would *not* do it before we could talk about what it would mean. Not only had Chelsea just been introduced to a magical world outside of Greek gods, but she was now a part of it. It was all new territory for her and something the beast would *have* to fucking understand.

The maenads sat on the woodland grassy ground, draped over one another, watching us with lustful intrigue. Some traced their fingers in that valley between their breasts, while others fingered themselves, getting off at the sight of us. There was a time when there hadn't been a night that would pass where I wouldn't fuck every one of them through until the sun rose, but those days became fleeting in the last decade. I'd changed. I'd transgressed. And the day I met Chelsea? My vision became tunneled only for her.

"I'm going to—" Chelsea cried, reaching for my hand.

Interlacing our fingers, I held onto her, pumping faster, harder, and making the satisfied sound of bodies slapping together. "Come for me, Red," I groaned into her ear.

My words sent her into a spiral, and she clenched around my cock, her body pulsing and shivering through her orgasm until she became boneless in front of me. But we weren't finished. Grabbing onto the dip between her hips and ribs, I held her tight, thrusting into her, tilting my head at the sky, feeling the pressure reaching its tipping point at the base of my spine. Just before it happened, I slid the rest of the way inside her, the bulbous part filling her, and I froze as I spilled inside of her.

Chelsea let out a gratifying, sensual cry when I'd pushed it inside her, her legs quivering as another orgasm waved over her from it. I pulled out, lifting her into my arms when she wobbled on her feet, carrying her to a leafy cot canopied with overhanging branches, and rested her there. Pressing my hips to her ass, I curled her against me and stroked her hair with my claws.

"Don't change back. At least for tonight," Chelsea whispered, her words sleepy and fading. Her eyes fluttered shut, and she let out a contented sigh.

Kissing the back of her head, I settled behind her. "I'd never change back if that's what you wanted, *mágissa.*"

This ritualistic act of mating was enough to satiate the beast—for now.

Fourteen

Dion

"Marry her," Bruce said, his eyes as wide as full moons, resting his chin in his hands propped on my apartment bar top.

Bruce had a point, and he didn't often make many good ones.

Shaking my head, I flopped my e-tablet on the counter, pulling up nauseating business spreadsheets. "While I don't disagree with you, that'd be moving a little fast, don't you think?"

"Not for a broad—" Bruce winced when I flashed him a glare. "—a *treasure* like that female, Dion. If you ask me, you find something that jives with you, and you hold onto it with everything you got."

I pinched the bridge of my nose because staring at numbers was already giving me an ethereal headache. "This coming from a guy who has dated a grand total of what? Three beings in the decade I've known you?"

Bruce put his fists on his hips and lifted his chin proudly. "I'll have you know I'm currently dating a lovely kitsune."

Pausing and giving Bruce my full attention at that, I quirked a smile. "A fox? You're dating a fox?"

Bruce waggled his bushy eyebrows and moved close enough to elbow me in the thigh. "Damn right she is, but no, whereas a fox may be her most common form, she can shift into about anything she likes."

"Good for you," I mumbled, holding my face in my palms.

Bruce tugged on my elbow. "Hey now, why the long face? In mere days, you found out your girlfriend is a mythie, had apparent mind-blowing sex with her you won't divulge, and yesterday, you took her to your fucking *sanctuary*, D. You've never taken anyone else there besides the maenads."

"I know, I know," I said, groaning, because what the Tartarus was wrong with me?

"Then what's the problem?" Bruce gave an exaggerated shrug and scratched a horn.

Memories of the way Chelsea had become so unbridled in my woodland retreat, her pleasurable cries, and how incredibly fucking hot she looked with her ass in the air in front of me consumed my mind.

"I'm not sure if she's taking me seriously. And I couldn't blame her." I beat my fist against the bar top, slapped my cheeks several times, and squinted at the spreadsheets again.

Bruce's hand appeared over the tablet, and he slapped his palm on it, sliding it away from me. "You're pitying yourself. You never pity yourself. What the fuck is *really* going on?"

Growling, I grabbed the nearest wine bottle and guzzled. "I think she's my mate, Bruce. But as I told you assholes before, how the hell would I *know* for sure?"

"The Crone," Bruce stated as if it were obvious.

I tapped my forefinger ring against the glass, relishing in its resonating melody. "Chelsea is supposed to be seeing her today. That's why I'm here *working* instead of wooing the daylights out of her."

Bruce flattened his palms, widened his eyes, and launched at me over the bar, bunching my shirt in a single hairy hand. "And you let her go alone? What's wrong with you?"

"Of course, I let her go alone." Frowning, I shoved away from Bruce's grip. "She wants to learn more about her witchy magic, possibly join a coven, I don't know. I figured she should explore *that* bit on her own."

"Got a bad feelin' about this, D." Bruce shook his head and slid the tablet to his lap.

"Why?"

My brain began to reel at Bruce's implications on what could go wrong during her time alone with the High Priestess. While Chelsea being a witch was great news for our potential future, it wasn't something I knew shit about, and I figured she should talk to the resident expert in town. What harm could come of that?

"What if she finds out the two of you are mates? She'd be finding out from that an ancient old crow instead of you. Think she'd be happy you hid it from her instead of bringing it to her attention?" Bruce interlaced his hands behind his head, looking pretty damn proud of himself.

Sneering at him, I tossed the empty bottle into the air, making it disappear. "You're freaking me out. You start dating one female fox spirit, and suddenly, you're an expert?"

"You'd be surprised."

Groaning, I lightly beat my forehead against the doorframe, my horns itching at my skull, the beast snarling for her under my skin. "Why would I have told her when I don't know for sure?"

"And that, friend, is called being a couple. You navigate things together. Understand?" Bruce poked his head.

"I hate you," I grumbled.

"Love you too, Beasty Boy. Now, why don't I do my job as your assistant, finish these spreadsheets, call the supplier, and you go talk to the witch, hm?" Bruce patted the tablet and wiggled his ass on the stool like he was settling in.

"Fine. But you are doing all of that from my club office. Not here."

Bruce opened his mouth to protest, but I snapped my fingers, making him disappear from my apartment before he could get a word out. I pressed my palms against the marbled bar top, my mind playing tricks on me, confusing me, and rattling my senses. I'd stood toe to toe with giant squids, fire-breathing dragons, and Hera. *This* was what frightened me. How did I tell the woman I was consumed by that we could, *might* be, eternal soulmates? And given my track record, would she even believe me?

Fifteen

Chelsea

"The horns, Elani. The horns," I cooed into my phone resting on the nightstand on speaker as I dressed myself.

What *did* one wear when visiting an ancient witch?

My sister let out a low whistle. "Since when do you divulge this much information on situations between the sheets? Or, in your case, the middle of the damn woods?"

"Since I've experienced the blissfulness of being completely unburdened, sis. I only wish I could feel like that more often." Getting lost in scandalous thoughts of Dion sinking to his knees between my thighs, the moonlight glistening off his horns, I rubbed the dip between my collarbones.

"There's no reason you can't. Sounds to me like you keep screwing Dion like a rabbit in heat."

My cheeks turned to lava pools. "Elani," I shouted, shoving my arm into one sleeve of a buttoned long-sleeved shirt.

Gurgles and coos sounded from Hedone near the receiver. "Please. The graphic details you just gave me on Dion's apparent beast form I can never unhear, sis. Never. Want to hear about

Eros's wing play?" The way her voice lilted at that last bit told me she was grinning wickedly.

Huffing, I slipped into a tan pencil skirt. "And I immediately regret telling you."

Riley hopped onto my nightstand, circling my phone before curling his body around it.

"I know, I know. Harm is off doing otherworldly war duties so I was your next choice."

I froze at that comment halfway to zipping the back of my skirt. "Elani, you don't really think that, do you?"

"A little? But honestly, I completely understand. Harm is closer in age to you, and *I'm* your little sister."

Guilt twisted in my gut, and I stroked my finger up and down Riley's fur. "I'm sorry. I never meant for you to feel like I go to her first for everything now."

"No apologies necessary here, Chels. I see this as my moment to shine, and boy, could I use the grown-up girl talk." Elani made kissing sounds, followed by Hedone doing a raspberry. "I also can't believe you're a *witch*. Seriously, how cool is that? Have you been able to use any of your magic?"

Tracing a nail over my lips, I sighed. The freedom of my magic flowing from me so effortlessly when Dion was there to remind me to relax was almost enough to make me kidnap him and never let him out of my sight. A grin tugged at my mouth with that thought because something told me he'd *love* that. "Yes. But it's only breached the surface when I'm completely relaxed or—" I paused, wincing at the *other* kinds of moments it made an appearance.

"In a state of complete and utter rapture?" Elani finished for me.

Bringing the phone back to my ear, I scratched Riley's head, warming at the sight of him smiling, his tiny teeth poking out. "That is a lovely way to put it, yes."

"I refined it for you. My mind was way farther in the gutter. What made you want to go see this High Priestess if you can't summon your magic at will yet?"

After giving my hair a final tousle in the mirror, I grabbed my purse and headed out the door. "Ouch."

"I meant no offense and certainly have no room to talk considering how long it took me to get a handle on *my* powers, but if you can't show your magic, how is she supposed to help you?"

My heels clicked on the sidewalk, the town's small, cozy vibes settling more in the daylight, brightened by the sun. "Dion suggested it. He thought she might be able to help me harness it. He said I should go alone because it was a *witchy* thing, and he didn't want to step on my toes."

"That's awfully nice of him." Elani paused and, with her voice muffled like she'd pressed the receiver against herself, said, "In here, babe. Talking to Chels."

Hedone's excited gurgling blared through the speaker.

"Husband home?" I bit back a smile.

Elani laughed. "How could you tell?"

I caught sight of the bakery shop where I'd met Sylvie days prior and halted. "I'll let you go, Lani. Say hi to Eros for me, and I'll fill you in on what happened tomorrow, okay?"

"You sure? He doesn't mind us talking."

The god of love never came between any relationships, but he put his soulmate's above all else. He made my sister so deliriously happy that I could only hope to find something similar one day, or at the very least find that sense of calm for *myself.*

"It's fine. Smother your family with kisses, and I'll talk to you tomorrow. Love you."

"Love you."

After slipping my phone into my handbag, I swung open the shop's door, smiling at the pleasant chime. Sylvie was at the counter this time, spraying and wiping down the glass display case. She perked up when I walked in and grinned like she recognized me.

"Chelsea, hello again." Sylvie's hair was down, this time in luscious blonde waves, the tips tinged a pale blue.

Fiddling with my purse strap, I approached the counter. "You remember my name? I'm impressed."

Sylvie wiped off her hands and put the spray bottle away. "Don't you remember mine?" A playful glint danced in her gaze.

"Sylvie," I offered, cresting a smile. "Short for Sylvaria."

She clapped her hands together and pointed at me. "I knew it. You seemed like a people person."

Chuckling, I reached into my pocket, producing a business card. "I should hope so. I'm in public relations. And this is a no-pressure-at-all sales pitch, but if you ever feel like you could use my services, here's my information."

Sylvie held it between two fingers and raised it, letting the shop lights hit it. "I just might. As you can see, business hasn't exactly been booming lately."

This was new territory for me. Do magical beings ask what the other was? What they could do? Would I be insulting her and jeopardize any chance of a future friendship or working relationship?

"Speaking of which," I started, tapping my fingernail on the

countertop. "I'm not sure how to ask this."

Sylvie folded her arms, a smile beaming on her features. "You didn't know this place was magical, did you?"

My face fell flat. "Can you read minds? And I'm asking that sincerely, now that I know what this place is."

Sylvie's face lit up at that, sparkling in quite the literal sense like shimmering ice crystals. "It's been so long since I've met someone stumbling into our little hidden town by accident who didn't know what they were. That's remarkable." She leaned her forearms on the counter and slipped a hand over mine, squeezing it once.

"But it *has* happened before?"

Before I became a more relaxed version of myself, her sudden forwardness may have made me tense, now, it made me smile.

Sylvie shook her head, her wispy bangs catching on her lush eyelashes. "Not since I moved here, but I've heard stories." She removed a tray of macarons from the case and set them between us. "And to answer your question, I'm a faerie."

Had I flat-out asked her that? I don't remember asking her that.

"Oh," I responded, leaning one hip against the counter. "And here I thought faeries had wings."

Nodding, Sylvie scooped a yellow macaron into her palm and bit into it. "I keep them hidden. They get in the way here. Want one?" She nudged the box of desserts toward me.

My eyes went wide at her nonchalance. And it wasn't as if I hadn't known winged beings existed, seeing as my brother-in-law owned a giant pair of angelic white ones that I'd touched on one occasion. Still, her abrupt declaration, despite being part of this world now, gave me pause.

"Oh, did you want to see them?" Sylvie stood tall, dusting

off her hands and working the remnants of the macaron in her mouth to swallow it.

Sheepishly, I combed some of my hair over an ear. "You don't have to."

"It's not a big deal. I forgot you're new to this, and I don't blame you for being curious." Sylvie flicked her wrist, sending a spiraling trail of pale blue magic that matched the highlights in her hair. It circled to her back, where a pair of snowy white and blue wings with icy outer edges appeared.

Involuntarily, my jaw fell slack. "They're *gorgeous*."

Sylvie's porcelain cheeks turned rosy, and the wings did a single quick flap. "Thank you."

The time on the cupcake clock hanging on the wall behind the counter caught my attention, and I sighed, knowing I was doing nothing but stalling at this point. "You wouldn't happen to have anything for courage in your delectable stash, would you?"

"Hm, I might." Sylvie tapped her plump lips, her wings slowly fanning in and out. "May I ask the reason?"

"I'm going to talk to Cressida, the High Priestess?"

Sylvie's violet eyes went wider, her wings fluttering quicker now. "Ah, so you're a witch, are you?"

"Does no one else go to see the High Priestess except witches?" I blinked, genuinely befuddled.

Sylvie scrunched her nose against her upper lip and shook her head. "Not generally, no. Between you and me—" She paused to lean closer, going so far as to cup a hand over her mouth as if the Priestess would appear in a puff of smoke. "—she's not the best company. Very serious, to the books, and a bit crass, if you ask me."

Well, that certainly didn't make it any easier.

"Thanks for the warning."

Sylvie drummed her hands on the counter and stood straight. "So, you're a witch. That's exciting. Besides Cressida, I only know of three other women in town who are witches."

"Really? We're not common?"

Sylvie crouched to a lower shelf, pushing the sliding glass to one side and removing a fritter. "Not in the Cove, anyway. But something must've *drawn* you here." Her faerie eyes flashed at me as she placed the treat on a plate and rested it in front of me.

My stomach twisted into a bout of pleasurable knots. Something or some*one*.

Laughing, I eyed the pastry like a treasure. "No kidding. I thought I was heading into Burlington, Vermont, to check out apartment complexes there and stumbled into this place."

"I do love serendipity," Sylvie replied, her shoulders and wings bristling. "Here. This won't give you courage exactly, but it'll loosen you up a bit. Think of it as a mild psychedelic or tinge of alcohol."

Alcohol. Wine. Was there anything that wouldn't make me think of him?

"Like ambrosia wine?" I grinned, my face heating as I lifted the plate to my nose, inhaling scents of butter, apple, and sugar.

Sylvie tilted her head almost inhumanly to one side, a charming smile curving her lips. "Not quite as potent."

After only one bite, I could feel my shoulders relax, followed by my mind. It was as if a giant, smooth hand coasted over my skin, soothing as it passed.

"You're very good with your magic," I mumbled through half a fritter shoved in my mouth.

Sylvie shyly found her ear covered by her thick hair, rubbing the pointed tip of it. "You'll find yours in time. I'm over a hundred years old. I've had *a lot* of practice."

I choked on flaky bits, pressing the back of my hand over my mouth to cough it out of my throat.

Sylvie jumped, her wings going taut, and she rushed to the backroom, returning with a glass of water. "Here, here. I'm so sorry, I keep forgetting."

Taking the cup with both hands, I took small sips until only faint tickles remained. "Don't worry about it," I croaked, clearing my throat. "I'm sure the High Priestess is going to be a hell of a lot blunter than you and give far less of a shit about it."

"You catch on quick." The front door chimed, and Sylvie instantly made her wings disappear in a flurry of snowflakes and light blue sparkles. "Did you need anything else for right now, Chelsea?"

Sliding the plate, now only covered in fritter crumbs, I shook my head. "No, but thank you for the magical treat. Time to face the music."

"Good luck," Sylvie replied, winking.

The new patron was a tall, muscular man with fiery long hair and a matching beard. A golden hammer symbol with a Nordic knot design on a thick chain hung around his neck, and he grinned at me as he passed.

"Thor," Sylvie greeted, her posture straightening. "What brings you to the Cove?"

I paused with my hand on the door handle at that, risking a glance over my shoulder at him. He was already looking at me and waved charmingly.

Dion had told me other gods beyond the Greeks existed, but I'd never met one. Arcane Cove only became that much more surreal with each passing day.

"Everything," Thor replied, turning back to Sylvie and leaning on the counter. "But right now, I've come to cure a bit of a sweet tooth."

I took the moment he looked away to exit to the sidewalk. There wasn't an official label for what was happening between Dion and me, but considering recent events, it was enough that I didn't need meddling with a hunky Norse god in the mix.

Considering how quaint the town was, it didn't take long to wander into the outskirts and find Cressida's hut nestled near a thick oak tree, as the instructions stated. I stood in front of the rounded, wooden door that looked like something out of The Shire in *The Hobbit*, clutching my purse's strap for dear life and willing the magical fritter to work harder. The relaxation I'd felt disappeared once a pane of wood stood between me and an ancient witch.

"You'll get no questions answered out there, Chelsea Stewart," an older woman's voice said from inside.

My heart skipped a beat, and I gulped before finding the gumption to turn the knob and stick my head in. The space was smaller than it had appeared from outside. There was a small stone hearth with a crackling fire at the back wall, dozens of herbs hanging from hooks on the ceiling above it. On the right side, there was a narrow bed with a purple and black patch quilt, the bed post made entirely of thin tree trunks and branches. Several shelves lined the opposite wall, filled with books, jars, bowls, and stones. At the center was a round, gnarled table littered with scrolls, more bowls, fruits, and a glass decanter filled with amber liquid.

"Hello?" I hesitantly called out.

I could have sworn I heard a woman but saw no one here. Given the very few places to disappear in the tiny space, she couldn't have hidden easily.

"There you are," the woman said, appearing from a darkened corner like a traveling shadow.

I jolted, my purse swinging, nearly smacking me in the face, and I pressed a hand to my chest. "You startled me."

"Spook that easily, do you?" The High Priestess came into full view, standing a foot shorter than me in billowing brown and olive-green robes, parts of the fabric twinkling with firefly light. Her hair was long and silver, falling in waves past her hips, feathers, and bone tied into several thin braids. The Crone's face was older but still strikingly beautiful despite the patterned liver spots and wrinkles overtaking her features. "Hm," she finished, hobbling past me to the hearth.

Ignoring that insult, I removed the purse from my shoulder and started to rest it on the table.

"Ah," Cressida shouted, smacking a wooden spoon on the table. "You'll not be mixing my effects with your own. You either hold it or set it on the floor at your feet."

Considering the purse was the only Louis Vuitton anything that I owned, I opted to keep it on my shoulder. "If you know my name, then you know why I've come to see you?"

"Yes. You're just a fledgling with no knowledge of how to use her magic because of your muddied head." She crumbled an herb in her palm, sprinkling whatever it was into a small pot resting on an iron grate in the fire.

Sylvie wasn't kidding.

"In a manner of speaking, yes. Can you help me?"

The Crone nodded, dusting her hands and resting them on her hips. "I can. But there's a more important detail we should discuss first."

More critical than manifesting my new power?

Fighting the urge to chew on my thumbnail, I flicked it against my purse strap instead. "Oh?"

The Priestess pressed her thin hands onto the table, pulling her face closer to me, the fire that dimly lit the room, casting ominous shadows over her face. "Be wary of the wine god with whom you share your bed."

Sixteen

Chelsea

Her words left a hollow pit in my stomach, and I pressed my hand there, my throat numbing. "I'm—sorry?"

The Priestess paused stirring to raise a grey brow at me. "Are you hard of hearing too?"

If this was what it took to get help with my powers, I might have preferred to figure it out on my own.

"No. I'm not. But could you elaborate on your empty warning?" Folding my arms, I struck my best power pose, rolling my shoulders back and widening my stance.

It didn't go unnoticed by the ancient witch who panned my posture from my feet to my head. "Dionysus isn't what he would seem. He's a trickster god. Has mischief in his veins. And you, my dear, are falling head first into his snare."

My nose twitched, followed by my cheek, and I dragged a hand over my face to still it. "He's been around for a long time. You assume he's the same man, the same god he was before?"

She shook her head, haughtily tossing the last remaining bit of herbs in her palm before turning to face me with a hand propped on her hip. "Gods do not change. Especially of the Greek variety. They adapt and learn how to put on facades, but at the end of the day, they are still who fate spun them to be."

An unease plagued my mind, and a dull pain began to form in my temple. Still fighting the urge to reveal my nervous twitch by chewing on my thumbnail, I rubbed the pentagram charm between two fingers. "How do you know so much about the Greek gods?"

"I wouldn't be the High Priestess of Arcane Cove—" The Crone started, grunting and wincing as she pulled a wooden chair out from the table to sit down. Her knees cracked and popped, and she let out a blissful sigh once her ass met with the seat. "—if I didn't have full knowledge of all its inhabitants. And the Cove has plenty of meddling Greeks in its midst."

A haze filled my vision, memories of how Dion talked and acted with me. He'd always been flirtatious, welcoming, and patient. What the Crone claimed didn't make much sense. But she was the High Priestess. Surely, she couldn't be entirely wrong, could she?

"I'd like to think I have good judgment when it comes to character. Dionysus has been nothing but kind and patient with me." I forced myself to stop fidgeting and pressed my fingertips into the warped wood of the table, leaning over it.

Cressida grabbed a bowl and jar of something black, emptying half of the contents into it. "And here you are, underestimating your power. You're a witch, dearie. You've been altering his brain chemistry without even knowing it."

My neck numbed, sweat beading on my skin, and dizziness formed in my head and stomach, making me rock back on my heels.

Altering his thinking? Was that *possible*?

"I don't know how to use my powers like that. I can barely summon them, let alone do something that diabolical." The words flew from my mouth in a haughtiness I hadn't expected from myself. "And you just said *he* was the one tricking *me*."

The Crone chuckled and grabbed a mortar stone, working it in the bowl. "Is that not why you came to see me? To learn how to control your magic? To use it?" She pointed a finger, wagging it at me. "And don't be so naïve to think that not a single witch in existence hasn't used her power to manipulate a person's thoughts. Whether it was for good or bad, we've *all* done it. You both are seemingly trying to out-trick the other, it would seem. Quite ironic if you ask me."

My gaze fell to my trembling hands, staring at palms where white magic had flowed from the other night. It had surged in sparkling, triumphant waves during that time with Dion—with the maenads. "It can't be," I whispered.

"Howdy," Dion's voice boomed from the door as it swung open. He flashed us a trademark pearly smile and glanced between us. "What'd I miss?"

My heart and core fluttered at the sight of him despite the uneasiness now consuming my brain. Gulping my nerves down, I gave him a grin and a tiny wave.

The High Priestess rolled her eyes and tossed the mortar into the bowl. "Have you forgotten how to knock, Greek?"

Dion stood tall, silently closing the door behind him and dragging a hand through his hair. "Cressida, pleasant as always. It's been a while, hasn't it?"

"Not nearly long enough," she scoffed, moving her gaze back

to me.

I wasn't looking at her directly because I was far too focused on Dion, studying him, questioning him, and desiring him all in the same breath. But I could feel her warning stare burning against my cheek.

"Missed you too, you old Crone," Dion mumbled before turning his full attention on me, extending his hands for me to take. "I came to check on my girl here."

"She's hardly a girl, Beast," the Crone seethed.

Slipping my hands into his wasn't difficult. Fighting the way my body wanted to sink into him the moment our skin touched was another matter entirely.

"She knows what I mean. Isn't that right, Red?" Dion ever so slightly tilted his head, those amber eyes roaming my face, seemingly aware that something was off about me. His thumbs rubbed between my knuckles.

My head nodded without assistance from my brain, and I pinched my eyes shut, looking away from him as if our gazes were what constructed this entire ordeal between us. "Priestess, can I visit you another time?"

A tiny smile crested at the corner of her lips, and she gave a single nod. "Of course. My door is open to any witch in need of help."

Dion's grip tightened on my hands.

"I need to get back to my apartment. Would you mind porting us there?" I asked, afraid to look at him and entrance us both in whatever spell I may have unknowingly conjured.

"Sure," Dion replied, rubbing his earlobe before making us disappear.

We appeared in my apartment, and Riley zoomed from his tower, immediately swirling around my ankles, working his way up to my shoulder, and nuzzling my neck.

"Thanks." Clearing my throat, I squeezed Dion's hands a final time and pulled away. "I promised my sister I'd give her a call at the top of the hour, and I would've been late. She worries, you know?"

"Yeah," Dion said—distant and suspicious.

"That, and I have a bunch of potential clients to sift through." I threw my purse onto the couch, snatched a pen from my desk, and used the butt of it to scratch my head.

Dion moved closer, his hand slipping over my hip. "I said I'd help you with that, and I still mean it, Chels."

It wasn't in me to pull away from a touch like that—sweet, calming, and claiming.

"I know, and thanks, but not today. Like I said, I need to call my sister." Risking a look at him and stifling a whimper at how devilishly handsome he was, I smiled.

"Alright, understood. I'll uh—" Dion squeezed my hip, and I almost told him to screw the call so I could ride him reverse cowgirl instead. But I didn't. "—I'll get out of your hair. You sure you're alright, though?"

Sucking my lips into my mouth, I nodded vigorously. "Dandy as a daisy."

Dion squinted at me, calling me on my bullshit. "This isn't about the woods, right? The maenads?"

He was making it increasingly difficult to suspect him of being a dickhead.

"No. Nothing is wrong. Really." Heat surged up my neck, and I only prayed the color wasn't showing on my skin.

Riley perked his head, turning it from me to Dion and letting out a tiny yip. I petted the length of his body to reassure him that everything was okay—for now.

"Okay, Chels. If you say so." Dion lifted his palms and backpedaled. "Text me, yeah?"

Nodding again, far too vehemently, I gave him a thumbs up. A fucking thumbs. Up. Gods. "Will do."

Dion smirked at my thumb, gave me one final look over, and ported away.

Sighing, I spun on my heel and flopped to the couch, slapping a hand on my forehead. "Riley, what do I believe? Did I bespell a Greek god? It sounds *absurd.*"

As if trying to answer me, Riley stood on my shoulder and patted my forehead with his paws.

"I have no idea what that means, but thank you nonetheless, bud," I said to my ferret, rubbing my face affectionately against his.

Grabbing my phone, I unlocked the screen and stared at the several text messages waiting unread—a couple from Elani, one from my dad, and one from Dion. I frowned and opened the one from Dion, curling my feet onto the couch beneath me.

Dion

Hey, gorgeous. I know you said you're alright, but I wasn't born yesterday. If it's something to do with me, talk to me about it, yeah?

Just talk to him about it as if it was as *easy* as breathing.

Grumbling, I let my head fall onto the couch's back and counted the ripples in my popcorn ceiling. What I needed right now more than anything was a distraction. Something else to divert my focus so I could come back to this particular chaos with a clear head. And what was the ultimate deterrent for one Chelsea Stewart in particular?

Work.

Opening a new text window, I feverishly worked my thumbs over the touch screen.

Me

Hello, Apollo. This is Chelsea Stewart. Are you ready to make a plan for success?

I bit my nails, waiting for his reply, and perked up when I saw the three dots bouncing as he typed.

Apollo

Wow. You even type like a PR specialist. You really are the real deal.

This distraction was already working and making me smile.

Me

I am nothing if not professional.

Apollo

LOL. Awesome. And yeah, let's meet up tomorrow. There's this new dive bar in the Cove I want to check out called The Crimson Crypt. Up for it?

A dive bar for a PR meeting? I supposed I'd met clients in odder places—the gym while they worked out, a public restroom, a hibachi grill.

Me

Perfect. Should we say four o'clock?

Apollo

Too easy. See ya then. ☺

Blowing out a relieved breath, I turned off the screen and tossed my phone out of reach on the other side of the couch. My emerald green crushed velvet blanket hung haphazardly from the armrest, and I slid it over my legs, sinking into the cushions to get comfortable. Riley made circles on my lap until contentedly curling up and closing his eyes.

I hadn't intended on sleeping on the couch tonight, especially not in my work attire. Yet, the mentally and emotionally exhausted part of me decided this was precisely what I needed as slumber pulled at my brain.

Seventeen

"I told ya. Should've married her," Bruce mused, stretching his arms skyward before interlacing his fingers behind his head, leaning on one of Hermes' cows and pretty damn proud of himself.

I'd swung by the Speedy Sandal as a distraction from whatever the shit just happened with Chelsea. One moment, I'm on my knees, lapping her up while the maenads made her feel like a goddess in my sanctuary that I share with no one else, and the next? She's distant, cold as a fish, and can't find it in her good graces to say more than a few words to me. It was our months' worth of strict texting, but in physical form, and I *hated* it.

"Shut the fuck up, Bruce," I growled, my claws and canines jutting out, the tips of the horns peeking through my skull.

Bruce's ears flicked, his tail going bone straight, and he pushed off the bovine, heading for the field gate exit. "Okay, that's my cue to bail."

Hermes came back from the barn with a hay barrel in his grasp, wearing only his pants, boots, and a dirtied white tank top. He raised a brow at a ruffled Bruce passing him.

"You're up, Herm. Good luck," Bruce grumbled before shoving his hoof into the gate, shimmying through it when it swung open.

Hermes moved his gaze on me, and I could already feel his judgment edging me on further—the kind of ridicule only a best friend who has been through some of the best and worst shit with you could provide. The sort of reasoning and common sense you didn't want to hear but thank them for later. But *now* wasn't later.

"What the hell did you say to him?" Hermes asked, tossing the hay in the middle of the field and using a knife to cut away the twine holding it together. He wiped his forehead, already sheened with sweat, with his forearm.

Irritation bubbled in my gut. "*Why* are you sweating? We don't sweat."

Hermes chuckled, flashing that award-winning perfect smile of his. "We can if we *want* to."

"Oh, you want to, do you? Hoping to have your way with me? Giving me a show?" I clicked my claws together, not bothering to make them disappear yet.

Hermes' smile faded, and he haughtily tossed the rope into the dirt. "I make myself sweat so I can feel the outcomes of my hard work that our godslihood robs from us. You *know* this, Dion, so what the fuck is going on with you?"

"You know what this is about. Don't give me that," I sneered, snatching my hand away from a cow trying to sniff me.

Hermes frowned and shoved me away from the animal, affectionately petting its muzzle. "Firstly, don't you take this out on my cattle. Secondly, yeah, I know this has to do with Chelsea, but I'm waiting for you to tell me *why*. Because the last I heard, you had an actual banging time in your forest with her and the maenads, and she was *more* than into it. Now you're here standing in the sunshine, *in* Arcane Cove looking like a lost puppy. So—" Hermes held his arms out at his side, the glistening sweat he'd summoned making those lean muscles of his more pronounced like a right dickhead. "—the fuck, bro?"

Snarling, I balled my hand into a fist with all intentions of punching a nearby tree but stopped short and let my hand thump against it instead. "She's gone cold all of a sudden. Can barely stand to look at me."

"That's weird," Hermes replied, scratching the stubble on his chin.

"I *know*," my beast answered, the depth resonating in my chest.

Hermes fanned his palms and slipped a rag from his back jeans pocket, using it to wipe his face. "Walk me through it, Dion. Can you do that without skewering one of my cows with your horns? Or should we take this inside?"

Grinding my canines, I jutted my head toward the building and made my way for it. I'd had enough control of my beast that I doubted an accident with one of the animals could happen, but the sun was stifling. Also, the less Hermes sweated, the better for my nerves since he insisted on conjuring it.

The cool breeze from the ceiling AC vents drafted over my face and neck, simmering the heated rage boiling in my veins. I'd closed my eyes, only to open them when the sound of the screen door echoed in my ears, Hermes following behind me.

"Alright, Hoss, what makes you think she's become distant?" Hermes asked, dusting off his hands and leaning on the counter with his arms folded.

Absently flicking the mail cubby boxes, I tapped a claw against the golden name plate labeled "P." "Her not being able to look me in the eye or hardly speak to me isn't enough of an indicator for you?"

Hermes slammed his fist on the counter, making a drawer pop open. It was filled to the brim with every variety of chocolate bars known to the universe. He unabashedly grabbed a Snickers, tore it open, and bit into it. When I raised a brow at his sudden urge for a sugar rush, he shrugged. "What? I did a lot of running today. I feel woozy if I don't eat sugar. Anyway—" Hermes continued between chews. "Do you think she's embarrassed about what happened? You said she's normally the shy type."

The way Chelsea had arched her back for me and presented herself to me like a female in heat had a disgruntled snarl vibrating in my throat. "I asked her that. She swore it wasn't. And we may have hidden things from each other a time or two, but we've never *lied*."

"What happened between the beastly bang and the sudden distance?" Hermes shoved the rest of the candy into his mouth, forming a large lump against his cheek.

Unease made my neck tighten as I recalled my conversation with Bruce about the godsdamned Crone. "She went to see Cressida."

"Alone?" Hermes' brows skyrocketed, and he licked excess chocolate off his thumb.

I raked a hand through my hair, tugging on it, the horns protruding further from my head. "Why does everyone keep saying that? Yes, I encouraged her to go alone, as being a witch is something for *her*. I figured I was doing the right thing by not stepping on her toes over it. Apparently, the fuck *not*."

"That has to be it. The High Priestess must've said something that spooked her." Hermes snapped his fingers. "Think she told her you two were mates, and Chelsea didn't know how to process it? Maybe she's scared? She only found out she isn't human like yesterday."

Scratching my skin where the horns refused to disappear, I shook my head. "I don't think—"

Before I could finish my thought, the front door swung open, smacking against the wall, the bell rattling so fiercely it almost fell. A hulking male tall enough that he needed to duck through the doorway entered, grabbing the bell with a wince and shutting the door behind him with extra delicacy. He wore a black leather motorcycle jacket, his beard thick and dark brown with tinges of red.

"Sorry about that, Herm. I'm used to the reinforced doors in our cave fortress."

Harkin. The resident wolf shifter who frequented the Cove but didn't call it home. Home was with his pack in Plena Falls, where he served as alpha. Whenever we were in the same space as the other, it became a verbal pissing contest, and today, I wasn't rightly in the mood for it.

Hermes slid between me and the counter, serving as a buffer with Harkin. He knew me all too well. "Harkin, what can I do for ya?"

Harkin wasn't having it. A smug grin curved his lips, gaze glowing yellow as he leaned to one side, glowering at me behind Hermes. "Dionysus, are you hiding back there? Afraid I'll bite?"

"Wouldn't want you to snap a canine." Flicking tree bark from my claw, I met Harkin's glare. "What would your pack make of a toothless alpha after all?"

Hermes sighed and hung his head, giving up and sliding to the side.

Chuckling, Harkin pressed his titanic fists on the counter, pushing his weight toward me. "Only half shifting now, are we?" He referenced my partially exposed horns.

Jutting my shoulders, the beast pushed through, making the horns extend to their full length. "I'm not a shifter."

"You might as well be, god of wine and frenzy," Harkin barked back, his canines enlarging.

Hermes slapped the counter, garnering our attention *and* growls. "Normally, I don't interfere, but this is not the day for this, Harkin." He glanced at my horns and back to Harkin. "Trust me."

Harkin smirked and scratched the corner of his jaw like a godsdamned hound. "Suppose I should take his word on that, considering how *close* you two are."

This son of a bitch.

Crimson crested my vision, and I dug my claws into the counter, already making my way over it. Hermes slapped the back of his hand against my chest, forcing me back to the floor. "He's only trying to get a rise out of you, Dion. You know that. Rein it in."

Harkin's amber eyes glinted at me as he chuckled before ignoring me entirely and moving his attention to the mail cubbies. "Any word from my mate, Malia? She went on a females retreat over a week ago, and I haven't heard a word since. They were supposed to be back three days ago."

Hermes fluttered his fingers until he reached one of the

compartments labeled with a "G." A blue light flashed, producing several envelopes. He shuffled through them with a cinch in his brow and slowly shook his head at Harkin. "Afraid not."

Harkin shoved his fists into the counter, cracking it. "I knew it. I suspected she might be rejecting me."

"After so many years?" Hermes asked but frowned at the destruction we'd done to his poor countertop.

There wasn't an ounce of me that roared to throw this rejection right into the wolf's face, but not only would that muddy my head further, but I had to admit to myself—who better to ask about the concept of mates?

Harkin snorted and dug into his jacket's front pocket, producing a cigar and lighter. "Mind if I puff in here?"

"Be my guest," Hermes said, flicking his wrist as if the place wasn't full of easily flammable parchment.

Having never been good at reading the room, Harkin lit up the cigar, the embers pulsing orange as he took several puffs and let it rest in the crook of his mouth. "She hasn't exactly been the best mate. She's quick-tempered, selfish, constantly trying to make me jealous, and has no interest in pack affairs." The wolf's neck cracked as he rolled his shoulders. "I'm not entirely sure why I was mated to her to begin with, but shifters follow the bonds. It's what we've always done."

Hermes snatched another chocolate bar from his stash with such speed my godly eyes barely caught it. "Can you be mated to another?"

My intrigue was building to the point that I might be persuaded to ask the shifter a question.

"It's possible. But I'll be a Lonewolf if need be. I'd probably be happier at this rate." Harkin removed the cigar and poised it between two fingers, using his thumb to scratch his cheek. "My point is, if she wants to reject me, fine. But I at least deserve the fucking respect of her saying it to my *face*."

Fuck it. Chelsea was worth the blow to my ego.

"How did you know Malia was yours?" I flicked my claw in the groove I'd already made on the counter.

Harkin arched a thick, dark brow. "Thought you said you're not a shifter?"

An ego was a fragile, petty fucking thing.

"Forget I asked," I retorted, turning away.

"For moon's sake, Wine-o, why do you ask? Hm? I'll humor your ass," Harkin countered, blowing a spiraling coil of smoke my way.

For several breaths, I remained silent. Thoughts such as would Chelsea reject me too if she was my mate? Had she had her fill after we fucked? That last one seemed absurd and very unlike the Red I knew, but I was at my wit's end.

Hermes kicked my shin and widened his eyes at me when I glared at him.

"You have a female you suspect to be your mate, do you?" Harkin asked the question for me, putting the puzzle pieces together before I had the balls to ask it myself, which further agitated me.

I gave Harkin a curt nod. "She's a witch."

Harkin looked visibly surprised, his ears perking. After blowing several smoke circles, he nodded. "Interesting. I wish I could give you a concrete answer, but it's different for all species. Most "monsters"—if you want to label us that—know as soon as they lay eyes on them. It's second nature. But like you said—" He pointed at me with the cigar. "You're something different."

A Greek god with a beast who was neither shifter nor monster—a fucking paradox I sorely wished for the first time in my clandestine existence that I *didn't* have.

"Tell him *why* you feel she is, though, bro," Hermes urged.

Sighing, I furiously rubbed my face with both hands. "I felt this strange connection to her the first time we met. I assumed it was the attraction. She's fucking hot, and I've always dug redheads. But she was the polar opposite of me, which made zero sense in my head as to why I'd pursue her. Yet, I couldn't stop thinking about her. I became *consumed* by her." A daze overtook me, and I stared at the wood grains on the counter, their swirling patterns morphing into Chelsea's auburn hair when the wind caught it right.

"You felt the urge to protect her? To *claim* her?" Harkin asked, propping a knee on the counter, a knowing smile edging his lips.

I narrowed my eyes at the shifter because I was treading dangerously close to having to tell him he was right. "Yes," I whispered, the word coming out more like a question.

"She's yours, wine god. Not a doubt in my mind about that." Harkin let out a hearty chuckle. "The real question is, does *she* know that? And would she even want you?"

Rage tore at my bones at the very implication, and the beast poked through. "What the fuck did you just say?"

Harkin threw his cigar to the floor, glaring at me, fur starting to sprout over his shoulders and neck.

Hermes sped to the cigar, stomping it quickly with his boot before shoving Harkin away. "Alright, Harkin. I'm going to ask you to leave before you two do more than make me buy a new countertop. I'll zoom your way if and when a letter arrives from Malia. Sound good?"

Harkin pulled away from Hermes' grasp, the fur disappearing into his skin. He pointed at me, the yellow in his eyes still brightened. "Don't think you're better than me just because you're a god. You lot are just as monstrous as we are. Maybe *worse*."

Hermes and I stood motionless and silent.

Harkin gave a final snarl before yanking open the door, not using the same care as he had when he'd closed it and pounding it against the wall.

Hermes eyed the vertical crack traveling down the door's center and pinched the bridge of his nose. "What are you going to do now, Dion?"

Cracking my knuckles, I forced the beast down, glamouring the horns and claws away. "I'm going to find Chelsea. And I'm going to tell her."

"Tell her what exactly?" Hermes asked the unease in his tone doing nothing to sway my decision.

"That's she's *mine*."

Eighteen

Chelsea

When Apollo said he wanted to meet at a new dive bar in town, I'd expected it to be your average run-of-the-mill Irish pub or even a sports bar with a dozen screens everywhere. What I wasn't expecting was The Crimson Crypt. The outside looked like the building couldn't decide whether it wanted to attract bikers or vampires. Considering Arcane Cove harbored all walks of paranormal and mythical beings, I found myself curling a hand around my neck as if that'd protect it.

There were several motorcycles in the parking lot, but not enough to constitute it a full-blown biker bar. Other vehicles ranged everywhere from Hondas to Porsches. It was still too early in the evening for the neon signs to glow, but something told me they would blaze in vibrant red. The rose logo dripped some form of liquid in cascading drops onto the bar's name, coating it.

Sucking in a deep breath, I tugged on the hem of my suit jacket, tightened my grip on the briefcase, and headed inside. It was just as divided as the outside with its décor. At first glance, it appeared to be your average American bar fare with a jukebox, numerous hanging TVs playing sports, and several high-top tables. Various logos and insignia hung on the walls—Harley Davidson, Triumph, Orlando Magic, Coppertone. There was no discernible theme, which led me to believe it was someone's metal sign collection or something similar.

The bar, situated at the back, was what drew the eyes—bathed in red and dark purple lighting, a giant blackened candelabra with lit, melting red candles hung over the black leather high-back stools. The bar was circular and deep mahogany, with so many rows of liquor bottles that the ornate Gothic shelves extended to the ceiling. No music was playing currently, only the overlapping sounds of murmured conversations and the different sports announcers on the TVs.

"Chelsea," Apollo's voice called out.

The Greek sun god sat at a corner table, waving me over and smiling so brightly it seemed to sparkle in the dimly lit bar. As I walked through the space, the magic flowing from every patron called to my power, tugging on an invisible thread that made me antsy. No one had looked especially out of the ordinary until I passed a table with two males—one had pointed ears with several small hoop earrings, his hair starch white, and his skin the color of a starless sky. The other appeared human, jet black hair slicked back with gel, sapphire eyes, and a charming smile. That was until a tentacle resembling that of an octopus, suckers and all, emerged from his jacket, nearing my hip.

Batting it away with my purse, I tilted my chin at the curious blue-grey tentacle. "You always let that thing roam where it doesn't belong?"

The man shot his gaze toward me and stifled a gasp when he

saw how close the tentacle was to my waist. It snapped back into his jacket, and the man bowed his head. "Apologies. They sometimes have a mind of their own. But—" He scanned my body, landing on my face. "—I can see why it was so intrigued."

"Thank you all the same, but you can tell your appendages—*all* of them—that I'm spoken for."

Was I spoken for? Was what I had started with Dion real?

No. I was not going to think about that. I came here for a distraction. Dion or not, it was as good an excuse as any to show them I wasn't interested.

The two males chuckled, the one with white hair more so cackling, and I sat at the table across from Apollo. Flicking hair from my eyes, I rested my purse on the table after wiping off something sticky with a paper napkin from the dispenser.

Apollo watched me with amusement, folding his hands on the table in front of him. "Is this like a ritual for you?"

Ritual. I hadn't known I was a witch except for a matter of days, and for some reason, that's precisely where my mind went first.

"Ritual? Like a spell-casting ritual?" I'd paused mid-way to lining up my pen, highlighter, and stylus to the left and right of my laptop.

The skin at the corners of Apollo's eyes crinkled, and his mouth opened, but no words immediately followed. "No? I meant, for example, how I have a ritual tuning my guitar before every performance. In fact, I do it *twice*."

"Oh," I responded a bit sheepishly. Glancing from my laptop squared to the table's edge and the tops of my three writing implements vertically aligned, I slouched in my seat. "I guess I never noticed I had them."

It never felt like that around Dion. His very presence relaxed me. He made me forget about patterns and worries. In the forest, I'd damn near forgotten my name and didn't care. It was just as they had described—unbridled freedom without judgment.

"Chelsea?" Apollo above the noise from the surrounding TVs, startling me.

My elbow slipped from the table, and I winced, also tearing my thumbnail in a painful spot from where I'd been chewing on it. "Hm, what?"

"Wow, where were you just then, Stewart?" Apollo asked, leaning back casually on his seat with his fingers drumming on the table.

Stifling a cough, I pulled up Word documents and spreadsheets for Apollo's Suns and separated them into equal quadrants on my screen. "Apologies, I'm not normally as distracted."

"Does this have anything to do with a certain wine god," Apollo asked, pointing at me. When my gaze snapped to him, he was already flashing me a snarky smile. "Uh-huh. There it is. Wait." He sat up straight, the grin fading. "He hasn't been an asshole to you, has he?"

Grabbing the pen, I began to click it furiously. "No. Nothing like that—or maybe? I don't know."

"How's that work?" Apollo pressed his palms onto the table and tilted his head to the side. "Not knowing if one is being an asshole to you or not."

My magic prickled at my skin, growing as frustrated as I'd felt, and I almost slammed the pen back on the table but stopped short and placed it. "With all due respect, I'd much rather put all of my energy into establishing your first gigs."

Apollo gave a disappointed nod and drummed his fingers on the table, a staccato-type rhythm only a music god could produce. "Fair enough. Where do we start?"

"You mentioned performing at Dion's—" Before I could get the rest of my sentence out, memories of him appearing behind me, his beard tickling my chin, lips pressed to the shell of my ear, tantalized me. Undoing one of my shirt buttons from the flush coursing my skin, I fanned myself as nonchalantly as I could. "—club? Bacchus?"

My flusters did not go unnoticed by Apollo. He appeared *amused* by them. "Yeah, that's the obvious one. But I was also thinking about this place." Apollo circled his hand in the air, referencing the bar.

After taking a quick survey, I turned back to him with pursed lips. "I don't see a stage or even a set-up for one. It doesn't look like the kind of place to hold live performances."

"Exactly. I could do an unplugged sort of deal with Raven." Apollo looked to a vacant corner as if he was already picturing himself seated on a stool with an instrument in his grasp.

"Who's Raven?"

Apollo sulked in his chair, the adjustment making the sun charm hanging from his neck catch the neon bar signs. "My acoustic guitar."

"Oh, right. Of course." I quickly added everything to the Word documents. "Do you play anything else besides the guitar?"

Apollo blinked before tossing his head back and roaring with laughter. "Does the god of music play more than one instrument, she asks?"

My face warmed, and I folded a strand of hair over my ear.

"Sorry. Prior human brain and all."

"I'm just giving you a hard time, trying to lighten the mood a bit. But yeah, I can play damn near any string instrument you throw at me. A few woodwinds, too." Apollo reached into his pocket, producing a yellow guitar pick, and proceeded to roll it over his knuckles.

"The cello?" I asked, my voice wistful.

Apollo clenched the pick in his fist. "I can play the *shit* out of the cello."

"I love the cello," I added.

Apollo raked a hand through his chin-length bright blonde hair, his glacial eyes glittering at my words. "Really? Would've pegged you more of the violin type."

Simply smiling to myself, I continued to type notes. "We'll need to talk with the owner about you performing here. They may not allow it."

"Turn down the opportunity to have *the* Apollo here? Unlikely." Apollo beat a hand against his chest like a gorilla.

Laughing, I propped my elbow on the table. "This isn't a mortal realm, Apollo. They may not be as impressed."

Apollo's mouth gaped. "You insult me." A grin soon slid over his lips.

"Do you know the owner?"

"I do. But it's still too early in the evening for her to be in." Apollo peeked out the window, the sun dipping under the horizon but still plainly in view in shades of purple, orange, and crimson.

"Not late enough?" I snorted. "What is she, a vampire?"

"Yes."

My fingers froze on the keyboard, and after saving my progress,

I rightly slapped the laptop shut. "I keep forgetting. This is all so overwhelming. I'm horrible with overwhelming. I start to stammer. I flush pink. I forget how to breathe, I—"

Apollo rested his hand atop mine, nothing sensual, just a reassuring, friendly gesture. "Hey, Chelsea? It's going to be okay."

Tears welled in my eyes because as much as I appreciated Apollo's kindness, I wanted that to be Dion's hand. I desired nothing more than to have those amber eyes gleaming at me with that warm and calming nature only he could give me.

Only him.

"Or maybe—not," Apollo said, his eyes widening at something behind me. He slid his hand from mine and slowly sat back.

"Apollo? What is it?"

Scents of soap, earth, and wine permeated the air around us, instantly making my core tighten.

Dion was here. How did he know where I was? Did I really have summoning power over him?

"What the *fuck* do you think you're doing?" Dion roared, his voice a beastly pitch I hadn't heard from him. He loomed over Apollo, who stood as soon as Dion approached the table.

"Dion," I whispered, wrapping my hand around his forearm.

He didn't look at me and delicately shifted me so I was behind him, his arm protectively curling me against his side.

"Come on, bro, you know I wouldn't go after your girl." Apollo held his hands up like this was a stickup.

Dion's horns started to poke through his skull, the claws edging from his fingertips. "Like that's ever stopped you before."

"Dion, come on, man, that was hundreds of years ago. We've both changed." Apollo gestured between them and then jutted his thumb at Dion's now fully exposed horns. "For example, when's the last time you showed those in public?"

Dion grimaced and shook his head like he couldn't decide between Dion or the beast. "You keep this strictly about business and keep your hands *off* her."

Frowning, I tugged Dion's arm, urging him to look at me. "Hey, he was only trying to comfort me. That was all."

Dion snapped his attention to me, poking a finger against his chest, his nostrils flaring, taking in my scent. "*I* should be the one comforting you, Chels."

His sudden possessiveness flattered me as much as it made me somewhat uneasy.

"You're making this a lot easier. Do you realize that?" I started to shove my laptop and belongings into my bags.

Apollo sighed and rubbed his forehead.

"Making what easier?" Dion's expression fell, the horns and claws slowly disappearing.

My sinuses stung, but I gulped back threatening tears. "To stay away from you."

"Chels, please." Dion reached for me but made no move to grab or physically stop me. "We've got a lot to talk about."

Hoisting my briefcase strap to my shoulder, I turned on my heel to level my eyes on him. "Yeah? We, as in me and Dion, or me and the beast?"

Dion's jaw clenched, along with his hands at his sides. "Both."

My stomach twisted at this, my curiosity almost getting the better of me. My magic had driven him to the point of nearly attacking his brother over me for holding my *hand*. This had to stop.

"Well, it's not going to be tonight, Dion." I flicked my nail over the cracked leather of my purse strap. "Not tonight."

A disappointed, heart-wrenching frown coursed over Dion's features. The sight of it almost fucking broke me. Turning away, I headed for the exit and didn't look back even when my heels met with the gravel of the parking lot.

Nineteen
Chelsea

I'd sat on my couch staring at my hands for a solid twenty minutes. I focused on intricate lines that made up my unique print on the palms, fingers, and tips. For a brief moment, my magic floated from my skin, and I envisioned it settling over Dion, infiltrating his mind and coercing it into doing my bidding. Convincing him that he was head over heels for me, that he wanted me and me alone, and that no one would come between us. These were thoughts I'd had numerous times, thoughts I'd dismissed as soon as they rose because they felt petty and selfish. Now, they'd all come true, and not even his family would come between us, which was absurd. What was next? He'd shun my sister?

Wincing at that, I finally closed my hands, tears streaking my cheeks, and a low sob bubbled from my throat. Riley had been curled up on my lap since I sat down, and he scurried down my thigh until he reached my knee, pressing those adorably tiny paws on each side of it.

"Maybe I should talk to the Priestess more. What if she can help me control this?" I ran my forefinger between Riley's eyes.

Riley bristled and patted my knee in his version of encouragement.

"Yes. Would you like to come with me this time? Apparently, a witch's animal companion goes hand in hand." Scratching his chin, I smiled when his ears flattened to his head, his back arching, and he started making those cute clucking noises he did whenever he was overly happy.

Sniffling, I gestured him up my arm and stood, grabbing a tissue. Securing Riley at the crook of my neck, I exited my apartment.

Unlike last time, no sooner had I approached the Crone's abode than the door swung open. An invisible force pulled me inside, and the door slammed shut behind me. Riley scurried circles around my neck in a panic before pausing on my shoulder and baring his teeth at Cressida.

"You brought your familiar this time, I see," the Priestess crooned while threading something on a loom.

My heart had begun to race but slowed, and I rubbed Riley's furry crest. "My familiar?"

"Yes, child. The animal who has bonded to you—" The Crone pointed a bony finger at my ferret. "—is your familiar. Considering they often help with a witch's magic, I'd suggest you keep him on your person as often as possible."

Riley's protesting subsided the more my nerves settled, and eventually, he curled his tail around my neck like a scarf and lay down.

"Where's your familiar? Do you not have one?" I asked after

searching all corners of the small cottage.

Cressida chuckled, working a wooden utensil up the threads, aligning them tightly together. "She's an owl. And I'd imagine she's off hunting at the moment. I leave the window open for her." She pointed at the cracked wooden window behind me.

Silence overtook me because I didn't know what to ask or say.

"Interesting that your animal is a ferret," the Priestess said.

I couldn't have imagined any other animal since Riley found me. "Interesting? Why?"

The Priestess stopped threading and massaged her hands. "They're known for their inquisitive nature and, interestingly enough, are associated with *tricksters*."

"Tricksters?" I half smiled and stroked Riley's fur. "Because he likes to steal things?"

The Crone moved closer to me, dissecting me with her cloudy gaze. "More like their ability to outwit predators."

My throat tightening made my magic pulse against my skin. "Dionysus isn't a predator. Not to me."

A smile crested Cressida's face. "Curious how you immediately assumed that's who I was referring to."

Agitation over the entire situation, the confusion of finding out I'm a witch, that my mother was a witch, and the growing bond I'd felt in my bones with Dion had my power sizzling up my spine. Bowls rattled on the table, the firelit sconces flickered, and the flame in the hearth lashed out, catching a pile of herbs on fire.

The Crone didn't look away from me as she slapped her hand over it, squelching the flame into dying embers. "Do you see now why I said your magic is swaying the god's mind?"

Riley nuzzled his head under my chin, attempting to soothe

me. "Then help me control it. If Dion and I are destined to be together, then I want to know that it's him who chooses me, not because he's—" I paused, watching my ivory magic wisp in sparkling tendrils around my fingers. "—bewitched."

"I don't know, dearie," Cressida tapped her longer fingernails together, shifting her glance away from me. "Such a power as yours may have no desire to be controlled."

Haughtily, frustratedly, I marched forward until only the table separated me from the Crone. "How can you say I'm powerful when I don't even know how I rattled the bowls or manipulated the fire? It was acting off my emotions."

"Precisely." The Crone smiled and used her hand to brush away utensils and a sprig of something, revealing a piece of parchment with a crescent moon illustration. "Because you're a moon witch."

My powers responded by swirling through the room, blanketing anything in its path with misty vapors and glitter that disappeared in its wake.

"I don't know what that means," I whispered, staring at the lunar drawing on the stained parchment.

The Crone patted my hand, her older skin so translucent I could make out every vein. "You will with time. Is coercing the attention of a wealthy Greek god such a bad thing? Even if you can't undo the spell?"

"Can't undo the—" I yanked away from her touch. "Why would I be okay with that? I don't want to manipulate *anyone*. Especially him."

The Priestess pounded the table, making me and Riley jump. "You're a witch. It's what we do. It's in our nature." Regaining her composure, Cressida flattened her silver hair against her cloak.

"Such are the burdens when our kind fall in love, my dear."

Love.

Tears filled my eyes, and I blinked them away, Riley using his fur to soak them up once they dripped from my chin.

This wasn't fair to Dion. Shit. This wasn't fair to *me*.

"You're supposed to be my mentor. You're supposed to help me navigate this," I croaked, my words crawling from my throat like a desperate, pathetic plea.

"What do you think I'm doing? You've already had your first lesson, dearie." The Crone flicked her wrist at the door, making it burst open. "Off you go. You know what you must do."

What must I do? I became more confused now than I was before deciding to come back here.

Numb and dumbstruck, I exited the Crone's hovel, staring at my magic still making infinity symbols around my knuckles.

My phone buzzed, and I fished it from my purse, frowning at the barren spot where the cottage used to be, the building now having disappeared. I ignored the name glowing on the screen and put the phone to my ear.

"Hello?"

A masculine chuckle sounded. "You'd think you would have your clients saved in your phone."

Shaking my head from the haze clouding my mind, I peeled the phone away long enough to see the name Apollo. For whatever reason, I'd been expecting to hear my sister's voice on the other line. "Apollo, sorry. I've got a lot going on. What's up?"

"I can call back later."

Riley curled around my neck, using his tail to make lazy strokes up and down my cheek.

"No, it's fine. I need to work, trust me." Following the trail leading out of the woods, I entered town, not knowing where to go. Home was the last place I wanted to be.

"Alrighty. I got in touch with Aurora."

I wanted to think I was good with names—no scratch that, great with names. So why hadn't I recognized this one?

"Who?"

A laughing green child with tusks sticking out from the bottom of his mouth, pressing over his top lip, sprinted past me with a chicken raised above his head.

"The bar owner. The Crimson Crypt?"

A bigger green being with tusks doubling the size of the child's and dark green, wavy hair hanging down to their hips chased the child, pointing a clawed finger and growling. "For the tenth time, the chickens stay in their coop, Benny," the being yelled with a feminine voice.

"The bar. Got it. Did she have good news?" I bit back a smile, watching the child and who I assumed was his mother. The child let go of the chicken, and they started chasing it around townspeople.

"Great news. She's not only interested but *so* interested that she wants me there every week. I'd say I told you so, but—"

Laughing, I walked further into town, stopping by the fountain in the plaza area. A bronze mermaid sat on a rock with her tail hanging off the side, pouring a vase of water that served as the fountain spout into the circular pool. "You can say it. I've got thick skin."

"Well, not when you take all the fun right out of it." I could tell Apollo smiled while saying that from the upward lilt in his voice.

"Send me her contact information, and I'll get in touch

tomorrow to see about setting things up. Sound good?" I sat on one of four marble benches surrounding the fountain, coaxing Riley to curl up in my lap.

"Perfect. I just texted it to you. Have a good one, boss."

"I'm not your boss, Apollo," I said, chuckling.

"You are. You'll see," he countered and hung up.

With a deep sigh, I slid the phone into my purse and people-watched. It was a wonder I hadn't noticed the eclectic population of Arcane Cove when I'd first arrived. In only a matter of minutes, I witnessed demons, orcs, and several types of winged beings I couldn't identify walking through the plaza. Despite the sun brightening the sky, the moon was still blatantly visible but faded—a crescent moon.

I'm a moon witch.

It unnerved me that the High Priestess chose to drop that particular bomb without further elaboration. Did she expect me to figure it out on my own? Was that how witches were supposed to navigate their magic?

I stomped my foot and secured Riley from toppling off my lap. He popped his head up and blinked at me, his tiny paws kneading my thighs.

I'd half expected the townspeople to notice me more than they did. Did they all know what I was? Did they know before I did?

I cared for Dion. I wanted Dion. I wanted this place and all its magic and luster. I wanted to learn how to use my magic and be the moon witch I was fated to be. None of that could come true, however, if I couldn't figure out how to control it, to use it, to manifest it fully.

If only my mom were here.

Twenty

"Tambie, when I said I needed a distraction, this wasn't what I had in mind," I mumbled, staring at the plate piled high with meat pies and four mugs of steaming coffee she had yet to touch.

Tambie tapped a petite claw against one mug's rim but still didn't drink it. "If you wanted something specific, you should've asked, D. Besides, who doesn't get distracted by food and caffeine?" She graced me with a singular glance. Otherwise, her attention focused behind me.

Scowling at my long-time friend, I turned in my seat, narrowing my eyes at Dagnar, the orc owner and chef of *The Minty Boar*. He flipped a towel over his shoulder before shaking hands with a customer who purchased one of his famous meat pies. Throwing Tambie an exasperated glare, I pointed at her. "You have the hots for Dagnar. That's the only reason we're here."

Tambie gasped and gripped the table's sides. "Will you keep your voice down?"

"Since when were you *shy?*" I snagged one of the plates because there wasn't a reason for *all* of this to go to waste.

"I'm not shy. I'm incredibly nervous to talk to him." Tambie scratched one of her antlers, her gaze damn near twinkling every time she caught a glance of the tall, staunch orc.

Scooping some of the pie into my mouth with an iron fork, I continued to chew while I talked and used the utensil to reference the overabundance of coffee. "Is that why you keep ordering coffees you have no intention of drinking? As an excuse to get a whiff of him?"

"A whiff?" Tambie rolled her eyes and folded her arms in a huff, slouching in the wooden chair. "Not all of us have a beast mode."

Shrugging, I combed a hand through my beard, ridding it of flaky crust crumbles. "No, but you do have a working nose, don't you?"

She went silent for a beat, staring at me like she was about to hate admitting something. "He smells like butter and pine, alright?"

Chuckling, I rested the fork on the now-empty iron plate and jutted my thumb behind me. "Want me to go talk to him?" I wiped my mouth with a cloth napkin.

"No," Tambie shouted, lurching forward, her cheeks heating when everyone turned to look at us, including Dagnar. "No, Dion. I forbid it."

Damn it all to Tartarus. This *was* distracting.

"You forbid it, do you?" Tossing the napkin onto the table, I pushed off my thighs to stand. "Now it's a must."

Tambie opened her mouth to protest, but when nothing but squeaking and gurgling came out, she sat back in defeat. "Fine. Please don't embarrass me, D."

"No promises." I winked at her before walking to the counter.

Dagnar snapped his green fingers when I approached. "Dionysus, right?"

"That's right." I propped an elbow on the counter. "I'm surprised you knew that, considering this is probably only the second time I've been in here. No offense."

"None taken." Dagnar let out a hearty chuckle, the large two tusk-like teeth protruding over his top lip shifting when he talked. "I frequent Bacchus. Hell of a place you run there."

"Glad to hear it. Other people's enjoyment gives *me* joy."

The words stung more than they usually did. I wanted to make Chelsea happy. It would bring me far more joy than the glee of dozens of strangers on any given day.

"What can I get for you? The ale here isn't mixed with ambrosia wine, but it tastes damn good. Perfect honey hops froth, too." Dagnar clapped himself on the chest with pride.

Patting my stomach and blowing out a breath, I replied, "I'm already filled to the brim from one of those pies, thanks. But I did want to—"

A female with pink skin, red eyes, and bleached white hair snaked her arm around Dagnar's waist from behind. She walked her fingers up his stomach and pressed her crimson, plump lips to his bicep, kissing him there. Her darker pink spade tail flicked and spiraled itself around one of Dagnar's legs. She was a female demon I gathered—a succubus.

Peeking over my shoulder, I slid to the right to block Tambie's view of the unfortunate setback. "This the missus?" I gave a curt nod to the succubus, who flashed me sultry eyes the moment they landed on my face.

Dagnar chuckled and kissed the demoness's cheek. "Not my betrothed, but she *is* mine. Isn't that right, Vila?"

Vila scanned me from head to toe, attempting to cast whispers into my mind. It wouldn't work. There were only so many beings that could manipulate a god's mind, and a succubus was certainly not one of them. After realizing this, Vila chewed on her bottom lip, seemingly *more* intrigued. "That's right," she cooed at Dagnar but still looked at me. She stroked one of his tusks with a single finger.

Godsdammit. Poor Tambie. The first being that she'd shown interest over in years, and this was what happened.

"On second thought, Dagnar, why don't you pour me one of those ales?" Sighing, I stood and tried not to look back at Tambie.

Dagnar gave a prideful, toothy grin before moving to a display with three golden taps and tubes leading to giant metal casks with wooden fencing around them. He lifted a mug, tilting his head to one side as he stared at the foam forming. Once satisfied, he slid the drink to me, and I handed him a lyyke coin, Arcane Cove currency.

After giving Dagnar a nod as a thanks, I sipped from the mug and fought back a moan. Fuck. It *was* good. I stared at the orc over my cup's rim, and he flashed me a pair of expecting eyes.

After wiping the foam collected on my mustache, I pointed at the ale. "Fucking good, bro. Real good."

"That's what I love to hear," Dagnar answered and circled his arms around Vila's waist.

It was a wonder the hulking orc was a retired warrior. I could hardly imagine him lodging an ax into a person's skull after making dough for his meat pies on the same day.

Tambie sat with her spine zipped straight, and she raised a hand when I approached the table. "No need to beat around the bush. I saw everything. He's taken. Moving on."

Slamming the mug down and purposely making her jump

because I was *not* having it, I leaned over the table and pointed behind me. "She's a succubus, Tambie. She tried to seduce me right in front of him. You think that's going to last?"

Tambie shrugged and flicked a crumb from the underside of her claw. "Plenty of beings try to seduce you, Dion."

I flopped back to my seat and snorted. "You're not wrong. And if it weren't for Chels, I may have taken her up on it to prove a point to both you *and* the orc."

"Ah ha," Tambie announced, pointing a stiff arm at me. "So, she *was* what this whole distraction business was about. I knew it."

Why was it that whenever it came to matters of the heart, everyone else around you fucking knew better than you?

I smacked my lips together and let my expression fall neutral. "You're diverting the subject."

"Damn straight I am. If Dagnar doesn't wise up to her succubus ways, then quite frankly, he's not the kind of male I want to be with anyway. I can wait." Tambie shrugged and propped her booted feet on the table. "What happened? Did she get weirded out with our escapades in the woods?"

I groaned. Tambie had to bring *that* up and entice memories to warp back in droves. "No. She was more than fine with it. She'd probably ask to go there repeatedly."

Tambie's brows quirked, and she flopped her feet to the floor. "Well, then, what in the Seven Hells is the problem?"

"I don't know." I punched the butt of my fist against the table. "She won't talk to me."

Tambie crawled across the table to flick me between the eyes. "Then *make* her Dion. And I don't mean hog tie her and treat it like a torture interrogation. I mean tell her you want to talk.

Refuse to leave until she does."

"Ow," I mumbled, rubbing my forehead. "I've talked my way out of harrowing situations with giant monsters, convinced kings to do obscene things, and delivered punishments I'm almost ashamed of. So, why is this witch so difficult for me to deal with, Tambie?"

Tambie let out a fluttering sigh before sitting. "Because she's yours. It's not supposed to be easy."

It was subtle, but I caught her fleeting glance in Dagnar's direction at that last point.

"Thanks, old friend." I squeezed Tambie's arm. "And I mean that. I don't say it enough."

Tambie giggled and yanked her limb from my grasp. "I said go get your woman, not go all soft on me, D."

"Fine." I stood. "But if this blows up in my face, I'm making you work doubles at the club."

Tambie's eyes sparkled like they always had when she was about to counter me. "And if it works out, you give me an extra week's vacation of my choosing."

"You know you could just ask for that? You don't have to bargain for it."

Tambie shrugged and stuck out her hand. "Sure. But this makes it more fun."

"Alright, you have a deal." We shook, and I slid the full mug of ale toward her. "And finish this for me, will you? Something tells me Dagnar will get more of a kick out of seeing you drink it."

"Oh, yeah?" A flirty grin crested Tambie's lips as she wrapped her hands around the mug.

"And make sure to lick the foam off your lips slow and deliberate, yeah?"

Tambie tossed me an exasperated glare. "I do *not* need you to school me on how to flirt."

"Sure, you don't," I teased, patting the top of her head as I headed for the exit.

She turned in her seat and shouted, "I don't."

"Sure," I quickly yelled back before ducking out the door.

There wasn't much I knew about being mates with someone, but I did know they often shared a strange form of unspoken communication. It was as if you had an internal tracking beam to know their location at all times. Which was great and all, but fuck if I knew how to *do* it. Pausing on the sidewalk, I closed my eyes and thought of her. My Chelsea. My wicked little witch.

It started as a tingle at the base of my spine, traveling to my head. Her voice whispered into my ear as if she stood a breath away from me.

"Riley, what am I supposed to do?"

And just like that, because of a ferret, I knew where she was and ported straight to the middle of her living room without a passing thought.

Chelsea yelped and grabbed a pillow from the couch she was sitting on, dragging it over herself like she was naked. Much to my dismay, she wasn't, given the tight pants and tank top she wore, but it was better for my concentration that she *was* fully clothed.

"Chels, we're going to talk, and we're going to talk *now*." I ground my teeth and swallowed down my pride. This was Chelsea. She deserved every part of me. "Please."

Twenty-One

Chelsea

I'd wished for nothing more than Dion to be here at that precise moment, and here he was. It did nothing for my fear that my magic was controlling him somehow. Riley leaped from my lap, circling Dion's body until he landed on his shoulder, those tiny paws pressing to his cheek. It was enough to make me wonder—Riley was my familiar, my bonded animal, so why was he so attuned to Dionysus?

"What do we have to talk about, Dion?" I forced my gaze away from him despite the urge to gaze at his handsome features.

Dion shook his head and scratched Riley's back. "Nuh-uh. You're not doing that again, Red. You're going to tell me why you're avoiding me, and we're going to talk this shit out this time instead of playing a game of who's going to cave first like we did for months."

This commanding side of Dion definitely did something for me.

"Why is this so important to you all of a sudden?" I stood with my arms crossed.

Dion gently moved my ferret from his arm to mine. The lightest brush of his skin *through* my shirt had my flesh sizzling at his touch. "It's not all of a sudden. I've felt like this about you for a long time. I didn't know what to do with it or what it was. Now I know."

My heart pounded in my chest, and I found myself taking a step toward him. "Know what?"

Dion bent forward like he was about to kiss me. His finger bopped me on the nose instead. "Why aren't you talking to me, Chels? You haven't even been able to look at me. *Why?*"

An overwhelming bout of nerves bubbled in my stomach, and I turned away from him only to have his strong arms coax me back to face him as he'd asked. "I think—" The words started but faded soon after from my throat tightening.

"You think what?" Dion rubbed my shoulders while Riley nuzzled at the crook of my chin.

"I think my magic is messing with your mind somehow."

Dion blanched, his gaze turning away for a beat. "Messing with it, how?"

And this was the part I'd dreaded confessing. It would be so embarrassing for him to know what he's been doing, how he's been acting, was all because of me and my unruly magic.

"Making you feel things you don't really feel, or acting on impulse because *I* wished it." Sighing, I let my head droop, my eyes focusing on my bare feet. "I've seduced you with my magic, Dion."

Dion let out a girthy chuckle, my body jostling from his hands still resting on my shoulders. "You *have* seduced me, Chelsea. But it has nothing to do with your magic. I've let myself be seduced because I wanted to be."

His laughter stung at first, but then what he said sparked confusion and hope. "What do you mean?"

Dion gripped my chin between two fingers. "I like you, Chels. And not because you told me to. Me. I do. And my beast is *feral* for you."

The way he wrapped the word "feral" in a growl had my knees buckling. "I like you too. But it doesn't make any sense. How do you know it's not partly my magic that brought us together?"

"Two reasons." Dion smiled and pulled me closer, holding me in a calming embrace. "There are very few beings that can fiddle with a god's mind. Witches are not among them. Not even Hekate could mess with me despite her trying several times when we were kids."

Peeling back, I pressed my hands to his chest. "What about Aphrodite?"

Dion frowned at that and uncomfortably rolled his shoulders. "*Are* you Aphrodite?"

"No," I responded, suspiciously dragging out the 'o'.

"Then, there you have it." Dion shrugged as if he'd just solved all of our problems.

Busying myself with combing my fingers through his beard, I stared at the small scar on the right side of his chin hidden behind that mass of dark hair. "You said there were *two* reasons."

Dion cleared his throat and motioned for the couch. "We better sit down for this one."

It wasn't often that anything frazzled the god of wine. Considering the way he scratched the back of his head and avoided eye contact with me, he was about to lay out something big.

Slowly, I sank to the couch, Riley scurrying to my lap, sitting back at attention for whatever Dion was about to say. "I'm all ears."

"You and I—" Dion referenced between us after sitting next to me but not lounging back. "—what I mean to say is—" He blew out a breath and fisted his hair. "Fuck. Why is this so hard?"

Reaching a hand to his shaking knee, I stilled it and squeezed. "Talk to me, Dion. That goes both ways."

Dion tensed his shoulders. "We're mates."

A breath hitched in my throat. My magic hovered over my skin, shimmering, spiraling, and I could've sworn even—singing? It was as if I'd already known this somewhere deep in my soul but couldn't ever make sense of it.

"Mates," I repeated, trying to understand it. "Like—soulmates?"

Dion let out a breath like he'd been holding it until I reacted to him. "Not exactly. Every species refers to it as something different and has different customs, but in theory, it's about the same, yes."

I scooted to the edge of my seat and took Dion's hands in mine. "But my sister and her husband are gods like you, and *they're* soulmates. What's the difference?"

"Well, you, for one, my wicked witch," Dion started, sliding a hand to the back of my neck and rubbing my skin there. "You are *not* a goddess, and since I have my beast, it makes this mating thing more—" He paused, tilting his head from left to right as if trying to produce the perfect word. "—carnal."

My stomach flipped over itself, and an instant wetness pooled between my thighs.

"How does it work?" It came out in a breathy, sultry whisper, my gaze roaming his forehead where the horns were hidden.

Dion must've caught sight of my longing stare because those same horns slowly began to make an appearance until they were fully poised on each side of his skull. "If we accept it, we'll share a bond."

I reached for one horn, acting on impulse, fingers gliding over the grooved ridges. I wanted to hold them while he fucked me sunken between my legs, from behind as we lay on our sides and any other way I could get my greedy hands on them. "That's it? We only need to accept it?"

Dion's gaze darkened, the amber in his eyes growing iridescent, and he yanked me to him, encouraging my legs to wrap around his torso. My core pushed against his stomach, and he snarled. "You're so fucking hot down there. What exactly are you thinking about, witch?"

Grabbing both horns, I pulled his mouth to mine, planting a quick kiss. "Tell me. There has to be more to it."

Dion squeezed my ass. "I love the way you take command of my horns, Chelsea." He lowered his nose to my neck, inhaling me and grazing his canines across my skin. "I'd claim you. Bite you. Leave my mark on you."

The idea of being claimed by anyone might have rubbed me the wrong way years ago. It might have scared me or downright disgusted me. But Dion wasn't just anyone. He was my frenzy god. My horned beast. My *mate*.

I might regret what I was about to ask later, but I had to be sure. "And you're positive this isn't my magic talking?"

Dion let his head fall before peeling back. "Why did such a thought ever cross your mind, anyway, Chels?"

Curling my hands behind his neck, I nervously flicked my fingernails together. "The Crone."

"The High Priestess? *She* told you your magic was messing with my mind?" Dion's eyes searched mine.

"Yes. She said I didn't know how to control it, and because I desired you, I was reeling you in with my power."

Dion's fingers drummed against my ass. "Did she say anything else?"

I rubbed my lips together, contemplating if it was worth saying.

"Chelsea," Dion beckoned.

"She warned me about you. That you're likely to stray if something did happen between us." I couldn't help but look away now, the very idea of it striking a painful chord in my stomach.

Dion turned my attention back to him with a single finger pressed to my cheek. "Do you think I would? The woman who has turned my life upside down, driven me mad with desire, and has consumed my thoughts since the day I met her?"

Tears stung my sinuses, and a grateful smile curved my lips. "When you put it that way—"

"Come here, *mate*," Dion snarled, using the back of my head to pull me toward him, fusing our mouths and devouring me with a sizzling, ferocious kiss.

Mate. I loved the sound of it and would make him repeat it until the label etched itself into my brain.

"Something's bothering me, though," Dion whispered once we'd pulled away.

"What is it?"

Riley squeaked and rose on his hind legs as if he agreed with Dion.

"That doesn't sound like the Priestess I know." Dion clenched his jaw and stared off into the distance.

"Do you think someone is posing as her?"

"In Arcane Cove, Chelsea, you'll quickly learn *anything* is possible here." Dion stood and held out his hand for me to take.

Riley bounded from his tower, hurrying up my body in frantic swirls before resting on my shoulder.

"Are we paying the Crone a visit then?" Slipping my hand into his, our palms buzzing once they made contact, I grinned at him, ready to take on the Crone, the world, and damn near anything else life tossed at us.

"You're damn right we are."

Twenty-Two

Dion

Chelsea's touch still left an imprint on my horns, the way she'd grabbed, yanked, and rubbed them. If I had known she would grow such a fascination for them, I would've shown them to her a long time ago—hindsight and all that bullshit. There wasn't a doubt in my mind that someone was impersonating the High Priestess. She was never one to meddle, especially with her own kind. Whoever it *really* was enjoyed watching others in emotional pain. The fact Chelsea had gone for days thinking her magic was manipulating me must have been torturous, and it killed me inside. I never wanted her to hurt or feel anguish of any kind. Even if my godly powers could do nothing to spare her, perhaps once we accepted the bond, her being my mate would help somehow.

I'd ported us to the Crone's cottage, making no motion to knock or announce our presence. I recalled Chelsea trying to pretend as if she hadn't wanted to see me break down a door with brute force. Grinning to myself with Chelsea close behind me, I slammed my shoulder into the door, cracking the frame and making it swing open.

"Oh, Crone," I called out, unleashing my claws and scraping them together.

I'd have thought her gone were it not for the bubbling pot of stew on the hearth or the freshly lit candles that had yet to spend even half their wax.

"Do you think they knew we were coming?" Chelsea asked, peering into the steaming pot on the fire with Riley propped on her shoulder, glaring at its contents.

"Of course, I knew you were coming," the being pretending to be the High Priestess croaked, shuffling into the space from a back room. "How else would I be the Priestess if I couldn't see into the future, hm?"

The horns itched against my skull, the beast begging to attack, to protect. If I wasn't so focused on the potentially dangerous fraud in front of me, I might have put more thought into forgetting the horns weren't hidden.

"The Crone is a witch, not a seer," I countered, my shoulders tensing from the unpredictability hanging chaotically in the air.

Cressida pressed a hand to her chest in a feigned insult. "You talk to me as if I'm not the Priestess. Whoever would I be if not?"

Chelsea slid closer to me, her hand finding one of my belt loops and hanging her finger from it. Riley, halfway hidden behind Chelsea's neck, hissed at the impostor.

"Why don't you tell us and save me from forcing it out of you?" I snarled my words, turning my claws so they'd catch the firelight, aiming the glint in the impostor's direction.

The Priestess bit back a smile and wiggled a withering finger at me. "Oh, now Dionysus, since when did you fight with your claws? Whatever happened to your thyrsus?"

Chelsea tilted her head at me as if she had no idea what a thyrsus was, and why would she?

Out-stretching my arm, I produced the golden staff of giant fennel covered with ivy vines and leaves, winding the rod and topped with a pine cone. "I'll most certainly beat it out of you if you prefer."

The Crone's maniacal laughter gradually morphed into a horrendous cackle.

"Wait a minute," I started, pointing the pine cone at the fraudster. "I recognize that fucking cackle."

"Who is it?" Chelsea asked.

"Yes, yes, wine god, pray tell, *who* am *I*?" The impostor widely grinned and pressed their fingertips together.

"Rumpelstiltskin," I mumbled, annoyed that the infamous trickster somehow wound up in the Cove.

He let out another cackle before spinning on his heel and transforming himself back into his true form. A pair of golden eyes peered beneath two grey, bushy, and high-arched brows. His deathly white skin was textured and grooved, with long pointed ears with several hoop and bauble earrings that poked from the sides of his head, a large, slanted nose drooping so far it almost touched his paper-thin upper lip. Rumpelstiltskin dusted himself and picked lint from his feathered cloak before acknowledging our presence. "You know, for a party god, you really can be such a buzzkill, Dion."

"What the Tartarus are you doing here, Stilts?" I hadn't lowered my staff yet, keeping the pine cone tip pointed at him in case he tried any funny business.

Rumpelstiltskin paraded the room, picking up random objects

to shove in his pockets like he was selecting souvenirs. "By here, I'm going to assume you mean Arcane Cove and not the Crone's cottage and to answer that, I'm not here of *my* choosing, I assure you. A sorceress banished me here, and hexed me so I can't leave. I got bored, and such a lovely distraction plopped itself in my lap." He leaned to the side so he could see Chelsea and gave her a fluttery wave with his gnarled twig-like fingers, black pointed nails forming the tips.

"Why would you say all those things to me?" Chelsea spat, venom lacing her tone.

Rumpelstiltskin tapped a finger over his thin lips and sauntered toward us, extending a hand to Chelsea. "I don't believe we've been formally introduced, love."

Growling, I shoved the butt end of my staff to Rumpel's sternum. "Don't you come any closer to her."

"Hush, hush," Rumpel mused with a toss of his long grey hair, motioning for me to remove my staff, which I didn't. "Put your knot away, frenzy god. I've already had my fun with her. I promise to behave."

"Your promises are worth about as much as a werewolf's promise to shave, Stilts." I jabbed him with the pine cone.

Riley stood on his haunches, hissing and baring his teeth at Rumpel. Rumpel snarled at the ferret, making him leap from Chelsea's shoulder. Instead of cowering away like any other small animal in the same situation, Riley snatched a small bread knife from the table. It happened so quickly that I barely caught it, and within moments, he was back on Chelsea's shoulder, the blade proudly clamped within his teeth.

Chelsea folded her arms, stepping to my side from behind

me. "Care to challenge my familiar still, *Rumpelstiltskin*? And, of course, I've heard of you."

"Ah, yes. From all the stories I imagine?" Rumpel leaned away from the knife-bearing ferret. "They only got about half of it right."

"You still haven't answered my question," Chelsea repeated with more fire in her voice, her stance widening, fists clenching at her hips.

That spitfire at my side was *mine*.

"Love, I thought it was obvious. I toyed with you for my own amusement." Rumpel scoffed, dragging a hand down the sad excuse for a grey beard grown on his pointy chin.

Chelsea took another step forward, and I struggled with an internal battle of convincing her not to provoke him or sitting back and watching the damn show. "So, none of it was true? None of it?"

"I wouldn't go that far. You *are* a moon witch." Rumpel swiped an iron spoon from the table, held it to the hearth's light, shrugged, and slipped it into his pocket.

Slowly, I lowered the staff but kept it poised in Rumpel's direction.

"How would you know that? You're not the High Priestess," Chelsea argued.

Get him, Red.

"I may be no Crone, but I *am* a warlock." Rumpel bowed with a flourish. "We appear to be woven from the same cloth, Chelsea."

"We are not the same," Chelsea spat.

Rumpel cackled, revealing rows of rotting, yellowed, and blackened teeth. "That's right. Because *I* know how to use *my* magic." He raised his hand as if getting ready to snap, and I lurched forward. "Ta."

I lunged with the staff but only met with air as Rumpel disappeared.

"Well, shit." Chelsea flopped her arms at her sides. "Where is the *real* Priestess?"

Using the pine cone to scratch my head, I grimaced. "Suppose we should've led with that one, huh?"

"Any idea how we look for her? If he's this powerful of a warlock, she could be virtually anywhere or appearing as anything." Chelsea paced a square on the wooden floor. "If only I could use my power." Frustratedly, she fanned her hand, sending a sizzle of starlit magic at the hearth, igniting the flames.

Frowning over her dismay, I lifted my fingers toward the raging fire, dousing it with trickling water, my maroon magic coiling around my arm. "That was a good start."

"I almost burnt down an ancient witch's cottage, Dion."

Leaning on my thyrsus, I tilted my head. "Semantics."

Letting out a cub-like growl, she stomped past me toward the door. "I'm going to check the surrounding woods."

"Then that's what I'm doing, too." I beat the butt of the staff against the floor, bouncing it into my grasp to use like a walking stick.

Chelsea whirled around, her cheeks flushed with crimson, lips parting to protest, but I stopped her with a kiss. She melted against me, whimpering into my mouth.

"Baby, I know you can fend for yourself, but I'm going to ask you to *let* me help protect you. Can you do that for me? Rumpelstiltskin is nothing compared to what could be crawling in those woods. Not everything in the Cove is righteous. That's the whole point of this place acting as a refuge for anyone magical." I lifted her chin with my knuckle, flashing her a pleading, hooded gaze. It was also an uphill battle trying to mask the unease I'd felt from a ferret with a blade in its mouth staring at me.

"Alright," Chelsea whispered, slipping her hand into mine. "We'll watch each other's backs." She urged Riley from her shoulder, encouraging him to stay in the cottage, promising that we'd be back for him. He whined, still clutching the knife with his teeth, but soon relented and curled into a ball on a chair.

There was no telling what I would've done if she hadn't agreed so easily. We'd yet to accept the mating bond, and already I felt such an overwhelming need to protect her—to kill anything who dared harm her. I secretly prayed no one would ever dare threaten her. Chelsea met the beast, but she'd yet to witness it untamed.

Twenty-Three

Chelsea

Night had spilled over the Cove from the time we'd confronted Rumpelstiltskin. We trekked into the forest in search of the Priestess. I wished I'd brought Riley because his absence weighed heavy on me. Today would be the last time we were separated like this. For an animal I once thought to be my adopted pet, he'd become spiritually bound to me. The more my magic settled, the desire to have him at my side increased.

"I'm not sure if it's finding out I'm a moon witch or this place in particular, but the night sky feels incredibly calming to me all of a sudden," I admitted, sighing at the way the moon's glow felt like iridescent velvet blanketing my skin.

Dion cupped my elbow and, not realizing I had closed them, opened my eyes. "Can you feel your magic more? The moon, the stars, it should all heighten your power if what Stilts said was true."

Pausing to pet a leaf covered in starlit dew, I smiled. "Considering how much he lied about, something in my gut tells me there wasn't a reason for him to lie about that a second time."

"Damn," Dion breathed out, staring at me.

I fought the compulsion to run my hand through my hair in case it'd become unruly. "What is it?"

"You're beautiful, Chelsea, but in this moonlight, you're drop-dead fucking gorgeous," Dion confessed, the word "gorgeous" escaping his throat wrapped in a delicious snarl.

Trailing my fingers up Dion's stomach, I landed on his chest. "Thank you. And as much as I want to have my way with you in the middle of these woods with the stars as our only witnesses, the Crone could very well be *another* witness. I don't know what I'd do with myself if she knew I delayed finding her, my High Priestess, to bang my mate."

Dion winced and scratched one of his horns. "I know, I know. I was only *half* propositioning you."

"By the way," I started, curling a finger around the tip of one horn, hissing lightly at how unexpectedly sharp it was. "You should leave those out more often." Grinning at him, I strolled past, letting my hand drag over his stomach, my nails catching on his shirt.

Dion groaned and snatched my wrist. "You're not playing fair, Stewart."

A twig snapped nearby, making us both stiffen. The mood changed from sensual to acute awareness within seconds.

A small brown rabbit with a fluffy white tail hopped from behind a thicket, its nose and whiskers twitching as it stared up at us with a curious gaze. Once satisfied we weren't a threat, it scampered along, disappearing into a log.

Groaning, I spun several circles. "This is worse than trying to find a needle in a haystack. Because at least the needle would be visible at *some* point."

"You're so certain she's hidden in plain sight. You keep mentioning that. Any particular reason?" Dion twirled his staff like Darth Maul in *A Phantom Menace*, and it had my core tightening.

After looking away to keep from being unfathomably distracted, I tilted my chin toward the sky. "Instinct."

Dion started swinging his staff haphazardly as if he'd inexplicably smack an invisible High Priestess and find her that way. The sight brought a much-needed smile to my lips. This was where Dion and I balanced each other. This was *my* territory. This was my moment to dig deep, find my magic, and save the day without ever raising a weapon or throwing a punch.

Concentrating on the moon's soothing light, I closed my eyes, listening to the air entering my lungs and escaping my nose. My magic flickered over my skin, but it was no more than a blip. It had no desire to do anything or answer my command. It was content on settling there, using me as a conduit.

If only my mother could have had the chance to explain *any* of it to me.

Mom, if you can hear me. If we have some form of tie beyond the living realm as related witches, I beg you to give me a sign. Please guide me in any way you can. I feel so—lost.

"Chelsea," my mother's voice whispered as if she were behind me.

I gasped but didn't dare break the connection by opening my eyes and checking if she was there, because I knew she wasn't.

Mom?

"I wondered if you would have ever discovered this about yourself. And for that, I'm grateful Elani was a gift from the gods. Otherwise, neither of you would've known about this incredible other side to life."

You know about that? Da never got a chance to tell you. He would have, but he—

Tears threatened, my bottom lip trembling, but I gulped them back.

"That is all well in the past, my dear daughter. I'm using what energy I have left. I've been saving it in hopes of this moment."

Can you help me? I feel the magic. It wants me to use it at my will, but I just can't.

A faint fluttering chuckle echoed in my skull. "Yes, you can. That's always been both your greatest gift and most debilitating curse. You think your hardest and never give yourself grace for not succeeding."

She couldn't have been more right because even now, I was devastated at the thought of already failing her.

I don't know how to do those things. I'm sorry.

"As a lunar witch, Chelsea, the night sky with the moon and stars is not the only entity that gives you strength. You're also attuned to emotions. Feed off of your mate's feelings, use it to calm your mind, and you'll be unstoppable."

A tingling sensation coiled in my chest.

Were you a moon witch?

"No. I was a solar witch. But it makes all the sense in the world for us to have harmony in that regard. That, and you never really were a morning person."

A sobbing laugh pushed from my throat, and a single tear rolled down my cheek.

"My time is up, Chelsea. You know what you need to do." A phantom wind brushed my cheek and I pretended it was my mother kissing me there. "Tell your sister and father I love them for me, will you?"

Of course.

When I could no longer feel her presence, I hesitantly opened my eyes to find Dion still swinging his staff as if no time had passed. Reaching out with my magic, I attempted to siphon Dion's emotions as my mother instructed. It started as trickles at first, threads of feelings but nothing concrete, nothing that stuck to help propel my power. I wondered if it would happen more naturally once Dion and I were bonded. For now, I surmised I'd need to improvise.

"Hey, Chels, maybe we should—" Dion started, turning around to see me launching at him with my arms spread wide.

I threw them around his neck, planting a kiss on his lips. He mumbled against my mouth, a smile following, and his free arm snaked around my waist. Dion's mouth moved in time with mine, and his emotions flooded into me, fueling me—lust, worry, hope. My magic swirled and ebbed, enveloping me until, suddenly, it all *clicked* into place.

The High Priestess sat on the ground, leaning against a tree not even three feet from us. She'd been watching us this entire time with no way of communicating. I peeled away from the kiss and fluttered my fingers, a white glow emanating from my skin now, my magic flowing and glittering until it settled over the Crone, revealing her.

"How did you—" Dion pointed from me to the Priestess. "Was it the kiss?"

"Partially," I replied with a smile. "I'll explain later."

Cressida stood, dusting dirt and twigs from her robes. "Finally. I thought you'd never figure yourself out," she said to me.

A white owl flew past us, resting on the Priestess' shoulder and nuzzling her with gleeful coos.

"I apologize. I only just found out I'm a witch days ago and hadn't yet gotten a grasp on my magic."

Dion turned to look at me with an incredulous expression. "Are you saying you *do* have a grasp now?"

"Later, Dion. I promise." Offering a reassuring smile, I squeezed his hand again.

The Crone stroked her owl's crest. "It is surprising you're so new. It has been a while since I've seen a lunar witch blessed with the moon's glow." She nudged her chin at me.

Glancing at my hands, there was that same radiance from when I'd used my magic to locate her. I thought it was connected to the use of my power, but it remained. "Is this permanent?"

The Priestess grinned and looked to the night sky. "Only at night. It's to announce to all other witches, warlocks, and sorcerers that you are a lunar witch with the moon's direct blessing."

Dion cleared his throat. "Where do I fit in with all of this?"

Cressida put a hand on her hip. "You figured out you were her mate far before any assistance from me. I think you know the answer to that, Greek god."

Dion and I exchanged glances, and heat built between my thighs.

"At any rate, thank you for finding me. No telling how long I would've been under that Mother's forsaken spell if you wouldn't have come seeking my guidance." The Crone scrunched her nose and spit on the ground, cursing Rumpelstiltskin under her breath.

"Are you still willing to give me advice, then?" I asked, folding my hands behind my back.

187

The Priestess scanned me from head to toe and gave a curt nod. "One, always keep your familiar with you. They'll give you insight into the world around you and heighten your power. Two, find yourself a coven." She shuffled between us, Dion stepping aside to keep her shoulder from colliding with his ribs. She pushed open the cottage door and stepped aside as Riley sprinted past her, the blade still in his mouth. He climbed up my body.

"That's it? How do I *find* a coven?" Disappointment laced my words despite any effort to mask it. I nuzzled Riley's fur, watching warily as the moon glinted from the knife.

Cressida cackled and didn't stop, moving past the threshold of her home when she called out, "Oh, they'll find you, dearie. They'll find *you*." Without another word, she slipped inside and slammed the door shut.

"I dare say Stilts posing as that old broad was far more delightful than the real deal," Dion grumbled, scratching his head with the pine cone tip on his staff. "Now that the Priestess is good to go, I think we should tell the sheriff about Rumpelstiltskin being permanently in town. He's not going to stop monkeying around."

Dion's words became an echo in my skull. I was too transfixed on my glowing hands and how satiated I'd felt using my magic without fear or restriction. And she said Dion, my mate, my fated mate, was the key to becoming my full lunar witch self.

"Dion," I beckoned.

Dion spun on his heel, tilted his head, and bumped a knuckle under my chin. "Yeah, babe?"

"I'd like to accept our mating bond. And I'd like to do it *now*."

Twenty-Four

First, I had the absolute pleasure of witnessing her fully succumbing to her magic, and now she took the reins about accepting our bond. I couldn't have answered fast enough. Plus, the way the moon made her skin glow gave her a newfound radiance she never needed, but fuck if it didn't make her that much more beautiful.

Without debate, I pulled her to me by her waist. "Say no more," I gruffly whispered, porting us to my home.

"Your place?" Chelsea asked, scanning the apartment. "I figured you'd have taken us to the forest."

Kissing the top of her head, I moved to the kitchen, rubbing my hands together. "Figured an oven and stove would be easier than an open fire. Faster, too."

Chelsea slipped her hands to her hips, the lunar glow still shaping around her like a halo from the night sky. "Why do we need a stove?" After coaxing the weapon from Riley's mouth, he made himself at home on the couch.

It'd been months since I cooked for myself, but given that I was a regular culinary connoisseur in various stages of my life I hoped it'd come back to me easily. Pots and pans clanked together as I searched for the right ones, resting them on the stovetop. "We need to offer each other food. Feed one another the first bite."

Chelsea sauntered into the kitchen, pressing her ass against the island counter and watching me. "That's it? I figured it'd involve reciting something or a blood exchange."

I paused at that, blanching. "Blood exchange, Chels? Pretty sure we've exchanged plenty of other fluids without having to get *that* archaic."

Chelsea flashed me a sultry grin that had my heart racing. A previous version of her not that long ago would've blushed at that comment. She seemed more relaxed now, more comfortable with her surroundings. "I figured that would be involved in some way too."

"It's not necessary," I started, twirling a pan by its handle. "But it'd be a bonus. An insurance policy, if you will."

"Of course," Chelsea added, playing along. "We'd need to make sure the bonding acceptance stuck."

Pointing a finger at her with a wink, I smiled. "Now you're getting it."

"I'm a horrible cook, by the way." Chelsea observed me whisking open the fridge door and selecting various items I'd planned to make a stew.

"I'll eat just about anything." With items cradled in one arm, I removed my head from the fridge long enough to pat my rock-hard stomach. "What *can* you cook?"

"A Hot Pocket," she deadpanned, her expression neutral and not the least bit like she was joking.

Shutting the fridge door with my boot, I blinked at her. "Like, in the microwave?"

"Mmhm," she answered, raising her auburn brows at me in a challenge.

"Shit. I don't have any Hot Pockets."

Chelsea chuckled and slid past me, hovering her hand over an empty spot on the counter. "I have an idea." With her middle finger, she drew a circle, swirling and swirling until her bright white magic trickled over the marble. When she pulled her hand away, a plate with a T-bone steak big enough to have come from a dinosaur rested there, along with a heaping pile of mashed potatoes.

The smell alone made my stomach rumble and drool collect at the corners of my mouth. "That's cheating."

"What can I say?" Chelsea pressed her forearms to the counter, bending over with her ass perked toward me. "I'm impatient."

Images of taking her from behind in my own damn kitchen flew rampant through my mind, my dick hardening in my jeans. I tossed the pan to the stove, not caring where it landed. "Fuck it." Using my magic with a simple snap of my fingers, I made a steaming bowl of stew appear next to the plate.

"Now *you're* getting it," Chelsea repeated my words back to me.

Cupping her ass, I moved my hand up the length of her spine and gripped her shoulder, pulling her face toward mine and peppering kisses along her neck. "You're insatiable, and I fucking dig it."

"Now," Chelsea cooed, raising the plate between us. "Eat up."

My cock was like granite now, and the ache in my balls had me grimacing. "No fork? You want me to eat it with my hands?"

Chelsea tilted her head to one side and dragged a finger over the curve of one horn. "I quite like your beast."

Growling, I snatched the steak from its plate and tore a hunk with my canines. Chelsea nibbled on her lip as she watched me devour half of the delicious meat cooked to perfection—nearly raw. She'd left no stone unturned. She scooped some of the potatoes with two fingers and held them to my mouth. Our gazes remained fixed on each other as I took her fingers into my mouth to the knuckle, swirling my tongue around them to lick the potatoes clean.

Snatching the bowl, I held it out to her, my impatience growing, yearning to feel that connection to her—the mating bond. She parted her lips, waiting for me to bring the bowl to her mouth, and once I tilted it, she sipped. The sensation was damn near instantaneous. Static wrenched my spine with such ferocity that I had to slam the bowl back to the counter or risk dropping it.

Chelsea grimaced, a small whimper escaping her throat, and she stumbled backward, both hands flying to her head. I snapped my hand to the falling plate, catching it and resting it on the counter. The overwhelming surges had come in waves but began to fade until Chelsea hunched over in what looked like pain, and my stomach clenched, a hissing burn dragging against my skin. That wasn't my pain—it was *Chelsea's*.

Rage catapulted through me, now realizing my mate was in pain. I couldn't rightly stand it. I wanted it to stop. Reaching for her, I clutched Chelsea's shoulders, rubbing them and pulling her to my chest, grounding her the way I had before. This time was different. This time, she was mine, and I was hers, and the soothing calmness only I could offer her melted over her the moment Chelsea's cheek touched my chest.

"I figured it would tickle, but I didn't expect it to hurt like a right son of a bitch," Chelsea said, her voice muffled from her face buried between my pecs.

If someone asked me to describe how a mating bond felt, I wouldn't be able to depict it in speech alone properly. Her breath had become my breath, her worry was my worry, and her desires were mine to fulfill without her uttering a word. The pain subsided, and I lifted her chin to meet my gaze, searching her eyes—they were still the same emerald green, but now the outer rim of her iris bore crescent moons.

Chelsea's fingers explored my ass and back. "Do you think we should talk to the sheriff? Warn him about Rumpel?"

Nodding, I slid my hand up Chelsea's spine beneath her shirt. "But there's no reason to go tonight. Herb forages at night."

Chelsea paused and eyed me curiously.

"Porcupines are nocturnal," I answered, subtly walking backward toward my bedroom with my mate wrapped in my arms.

Chelsea shrugged as if this information were now commonplace. It drove me wild that my *mate* was in the Cove. That fate brought us together in the craziest of fucking ways, especially when I had never thought or imagined the universe would ever put me in someone's path, let alone the gem that Chelsea was.

"Tomorrow morning, then?" Chelsea smiled, her palm splaying between my shoulders, that moon magic encircling my torso and making my clothes disintegrate.

Digging my claws into Chelsea's shirt and pants, gathering them in a bunch, I tore them away using a combination of my magic and the beast. "Tomorrow."

Chelsea grinned and backpedaled until she reached my king-size bed covered in black and red wine silk sheets and pillows. She slid her ass across it, crooking her finger at me, beckoning me, and ever so slowly parting her knees to show me my bonding present.

Sinking to my hands and knees, I crawled over to her, slipping between her thighs, my cock sliding over her wetness. In one swift movement that caught me for a godsdamned whirl, Chelsea wrapped her hand around the back of my neck and flipped us. She sat on top of me, grinding her clit against my shaft, shivering when it hit the ridge.

Smiling at her, I moved one hand behind my head, using the other to roam her porcelain curves. "Fuck me, Red."

She scraped her nails down my chest, her ivory magic gliding over my skin, our new bond making the sensation fucking tantalizing. I groaned and bucked my hips, enticing a wicked grin to crest Chelsea's lips. She reached between her legs and positioned me at her entrance before slowly lowering herself, purposely letting inch by inch of me fill her. I grabbed her hip, gritting my teeth and shoving the back of my head into the pillows. She hadn't started to move yet, and it was easily the most pleasurable thing I'd felt in my ethereal life.

Fucking had always been about carnal pleasure for me—an itch to scratch. It hadn't ever meant anything beyond physical satiation. With Chelsea, it satisfied an entirely different side of me. I *cherished* the woman writhing on top of me. The universe be damned for anyone who'd try to harm her.

When her hips met mine, she began to rock, rolling herself up, down, forward, and back, clenching herself around my cock, damn near strangling it. The moon peeked through the shimmering, opaque black curtains hanging over my front bay window and blessed her with its glow. Chelsea gyrated and bucked, my hand kneading one breast and tweaking the nipple while *her* hand massaged the other. Her hands moved to her fiery tendrils, bunching them in disarray atop her head.

One look at her, and it was a fucking mystery how she wasn't a goddess in her own right. I'd been with so many beings through the ages that it gave me a strange sense of guilt that none of them were her. Damn. Was this what it felt like to *fall*? To step off the ledge, unafraid, knowing the other person will catch you?

The tingle began to form at the base of my spine, and I grabbed her, willing her to hold still for a moment to gather myself, but she refused. Chelsea swatted my hand away and leaned over me, her breasts brushing my chest.

"Not every time we fuck does it have to be a marathon, Dion. Even for you," she whispered, still rubbing herself expertly against me. "So come with me, frenzy god."

My beast snarled in approval of my mate's courage to take control. I playfully nipped the air in front of her face. "My wicked. Little. Witch." Taking one of her hands, I placed it on a horn and moaned as my climax built, my balls tightening to the point of blissful agony.

With her silky hand stroking my horn and after several more rolls of her hips, her back arched, *screaming* as she came. Grunting, I spilled inside her a breath later, my beast roaring, arms and legs stiffening, and her grip tightening on my horn, intensifying it, had me *growling*.

Sheening with sweat and her flowered scent permeating the air between us, Chelsea fell in a boneless heap beside me, a tired smile gracing her lips. "You look like you have something on your mind, Dion."

Tracing her jawline from one end to the other, I propped my head in my hand. "I just realized that you haven't smoked since the day I first ran into you in the Cove."

"You're right." Chelsea's eyes fluttered as realization dawned on her. "I haven't had the urge." Her gaze grew sultry and hooded. "Guess I simply needed a better distraction."

I cupped her chin with one hand, minding my claws, and kissed her.

"You're *mine*, Dionysus," she whispered, the satiation melting over her features bringing me a sense of accomplishment—a deed that'd make me sleep better for it.

Hitching one leg over her, I used it to pull her closer, stroking my thumb over her flushed cheek. "I'm yours, mate. All *yours*."

Twenty-Five

Chelsea

Invigorating. There was no other word I could think of to describe the way being bonded to Dion made me feel. I never realized how incomplete I was until accepting the bond with him. I'd thought it was due to my wiry personality and tendencies to overthink everything in my life, but those hadn't. I think that was the best part about this entire situation. Not only did I inherit a mate, a lifelong partner, but I didn't lose any of myself in the process. I'm a better version of myself with him, and I'd found my *true* self as a lunar witch.

I'd awoken the next day curled into my mate's arms, my hand lazily dangling from one of his horns. I'd be lying if I said I wasn't extremely fascinated by them. It also astounded me that he felt compelled to keep them hidden until recently, as if the sight of them would appall me when I positively *loved* them. We'd made love again because we couldn't seem to get enough of each other before Dion ported us to the sheriff's office soon after.

I wasn't sure what I was expecting it to look like, but I didn't imagine something out of the American Old West. It was a quaint building with wooden paneling and three posts holding up the shingle overhang above a dark brown door. The word "sheriff" was displayed in all capital letters in the same font one would associate with the Old West. A stone chimney puffed smoke from the roof, and wooden stairs with a simple banister led to a second floor of an attached part of the building. A giant oak tree shaded the building with its vibrant green leaves and sturdy trunk.

As we made for the entrance, I pointed at a hitching post. "Is that for a horse? Does he ride?"

Dion shrugged and held the door open for me. "Herb's an older soul, if you couldn't tell by the building design, and doesn't own a car, so I'd say yes."

"He doesn't ride it in porcupine form, does he? I feel like that'd be dangerous for the horse?" I asked, the absurdity of how it sounded out loud no longer phasing me.

Once I stepped inside, Dion entered behind me, chuckling. "I'd like to see him not only mount a horse but stay on the saddle as a fucking porcupine."

"Don't you go pokin' fun at me, boy. I'll quill your ass," a gruff male voice thick with an American southern accent said.

Dion leaned on one of two wooden pillars situated between several desks, chairs, and a wall of four separate holding cells. "Pipe down, you prickly old timer. It's called a joke."

A shorter male, standing a height between me and Dion, emerged from a backroom, his gait wide as he walked, legs slightly bowed. He wore a tan ten-gallon hat, dark blue duster, boots with spurs, and a silver sheriff's star pinned to his blue filigree satin vest. A leather belt slung over his hips, a single six-shooter hanging on his left side. He had his thumbs hanging from the belt, and if a human could ever look somehow like a porcupine at the same time, that would be Herb. His nose was broad and close to his face, nostrils thin and the width of his nose. Herb's eyes were so dark they almost appeared one color, glossy, with wrinkled eyelids. The way his salt and pepper mustache stretched to each side simulated quills.

"Lookie you with your bits out." Herb pointed at Dion's prominently displayed horns.

I couldn't be certain if it was my pride for his horns or his, given our connection now, but I had to pin my thighs together when he stroked one with a smug grin.

"Figured it was about time. Besides, they itch like a flea-infested werewolf when I keep them hidden." Dion winced and scratched where the horn met his forehead.

Already missing his skin pressed to mine, I curled my arm through Dion's and brushed our shoulders. Dion kissed the side of my head.

"Well, to what pleasure do I owe this rare visit, Dion?" Herb hitched his belt, and his wiry mustache bristled.

"We wanted to warn you that Rumpelstiltskin is in town for the foreseeable future," Dion answered, his hand finding my lower back and pressing his palm there in a claiming gesture.

"Rumpelstiltskin? What in tarnation is that meddling warlock doing in the Cove? Figured he'd hate it here." Herb shuffled through papers chaotically sprawled on a desk at the head of the room.

"He's been cursed and apparently can't leave here unless the sorceress lifts it. Be prepared for a lot of complaints."

Herb's wide, stubby nose twitched as he nodded. "I see, I see. I'll keep it in mind. But I'm afraid there's much bigger fish to fry than a trickster playing a few pranks now and again."

Dion's hand stiffened at my back. "What do you mean?"

"A pixie was murdered last night." The hair sprouting from Herb's head hardened and raised.

"Murder? Here?" Dion pointed at the floor, surprise evident in his tone.

"Not here in the sheriff's office, but out in the woods where they host their little festivities." Herb jutted his thumb behind him.

"I didn't mean here as in *right* here, Herb. I meant the Cove. There hasn't been a murder reported in years, right?" Dion asked, his growing impatience stirring anxiety in my gut.

Herb shifted the hat back far enough for him to scratch his head. "Last I can recall is when that wraith went rabid, and that was over two years ago. Plenty of bad eggs here, but not murderous ones."

"Any witnesses?" I asked, my magic humming, desiring to help.

Herb shook his head. "If there was, none have come forward."

"Wait a minute," Dion started, snapping his fingers. "Do you know who else is new to town besides Stilts? Erebus."

Herb's black orbed eyes widened. "That shadowy feller?"

"Yeah. He ran an organized crime ring in Chicago before moving here. No telling what shit he's already managed to get into." Dion wrapped a hand over the grape charm on his necklace.

Fury built between us, *all* of it emanating from my frenzy god. I slipped a hand over his shoulder to calm him.

"I'll talk to him, Herb. If he's behind this, I'll get it out of him even if I have to filet him with my horns." Dion's lip bounced in a snarl.

"Now, there's no need for you to get mixed up in all this, Dion.

I'm the sheriff and I can handle it." Herb shuffled toward an old rotary phone hanging on the wall.

"It's not a big deal, Herb. Bus and I go way back in the worst of ways. I'll let you know what I find out." Dion held his hand out to me, leading us toward the exit.

Once outside, I rubbed my arms, an eerie chill washing over me from the idea of someone being murdered in the town I now called home. "Something's bothering me, D."

"What is it?" Dion cupped my elbow.

"We chose not to go to Herb last night to fucking each other's brains out instead. Someone was murdered while I was riding you, Dion."

My magic pulsed from my skin, reacting to the guilt I felt.

Dion frowned and traced my jawline with his thumb. "Don't go thinking in hindsight about something like this, Red. How the shit were we supposed to know that was going to happen?"

Sighing, because I knew he was right, I hugged myself tighter. "If only I'd been given seer powers."

"Would you honestly want that? The ability to see into the future? Sure, I guess it'd help in the grand scheme of things, but then there'd be no more surprises." Dion traced his fingers through my hair, catching on a knot that he took care to comb through.

"I know, I know. I can't help feeling guilty now that I can use my magic. Not that I'm sure what I would've done to stop it if I didn't know it was going to happen." A frustrated snarl tickled my throat, and I fought the urge to stomp my foot.

"Come here, mate," Dion beckoned with burly, open arms.

I hugged him and pressed my ear to his chest, calming myself to the sound of his strong, godly heartbeat.

"Chelsea Stewart?" An unfamiliar female voice called out.

"Who wants to know?" Dion asked in a gruff, protective tone.

Lifting my head, I squeezed Dion's shoulder. Two women in dark grey dresses and hooded black cloaks stood on the other side of the dirt path. They both had long, wavy chestnut hair, and their facial features were so similar I wondered if they were sisters.

My magic settled over my mind, a similar surge of power emanating from the two women but in different harmony from mine.

Witches.

Moving from behind Dion's body shield, I gripped his bicep. "They're witches."

Dion blinked, and his predatory demeanor relaxed, his shoulders lowering from his ears, hands resting at his sides.

"Yes? That's me," I answered, still approaching with caution.

The taller of the two women lowered her hood and took a step forward. Her jawline was angular, matching the lengthy swoop of her nose. Her sapphire gaze caught with mine. and I couldn't decipher if her expression were of sadness or hesitation. "We wish to speak with you about the possibility of joining our coven."

My heart fluttered at that prospect.

The other woman stepped beside her but didn't remove her hood. "Something unfortunately took our third from us last night."

The pixie. She was a witch.

Guilt tried to gnaw at my bones again. Had fate swapped the pixie's life for mine to give me a coven? At sisterhood? And if so, *why* me?

The two witches stared at me in desperate silence. The still hooded woman had dark circles under her eyes like she'd been crying, the tip of her nose rosy red.

Looking at Dion, I parted my lips to ask him what he made of this, but he answered before I could edge a word out.

"You should hear what they have to say, Chels. This could be good for you. I need to go talk to Erebus anyway." Dion shrugged and gave that snarky smile, suggesting that none of this would come between us.

"You sure?"

"Yes," he whispered, kissing my cheek. "Meet me at the club when you're done, alright?" Dion waved at the other witches. "Be nice to her, will you?"

"She's our sister, wine god," the taller woman answered. "We'd never wish any ill-will toward her, no matter her decision."

"Your mate will be safe," the quiet one added.

With a tensed jaw, Dion nodded and gave me one final glance with his captivating amber eyes before porting away.

Twenty-Six

Arcane Cove was welcoming. The Cove didn't turn any magical or mythical being away. It had never been an issue when heroes and villains could coexist without dipping into each other's affairs in neutral territory—until now. Someone had to stir the pot after all this time. Someone felt compelled to start a ripple that wouldn't be easy to bounce back from. And I'd bet my right horn that someone was a shadow god with an affection for black.

Tambie had reported Erebus practically making camp inside my club in the same booth. At first, I'd thought nothing of it, especially given how much scratch he paid for the accommodations. The thought of him conducting business inside *my* establishment and all of it possibly connected to the death of a mythie, however? That I couldn't ignore.

It took all of my inner strength not to throw the table, drinks still perched on it, when I'd ported into the lounge area. I puffed my chest and held my claws poised at my sides, ready to slash and gash if necessary.

Erebus sat in the center surrounded by his usual goons, puffing on a cigar with his elbow propped and that same satisfied, smug-ass grin. His onyx eyes darted to my displayed horns, and he smirked. "Something on your mind, Dion?"

"You've got a lot of balls, primordial." The words came out gritty and clipped because I couldn't manage to unclench my jaw from spiraling fury.

Erebus sighed and flicked cigar ash into a glass tray. "Care to give a little more context, or would you rather me go into tales of precisely *how* big my balls are?"

Pulling on my mating bond with Chelsea, I let her calmer nature soothe me, hoping my rage wasn't affecting her with a potential coven. "I warned you that if you went too far with your mafia bullshit, I'd see your ass out of the Cove." I pointed a claw in his face.

Erebus glared at me and gave one head flick to send his posse packing. With a tense jaw, he put out the cigar and adjusted his black suit jacket, his inky shadows already framing him. "All I've done since setting up shop here, Dionysus, is starting a ring for pixie sticks."

Pixie sticks—not the mortal childhood favorite candy of sugary, fruity powder you poured on your tongue. In the Cove, beings quickly realized that the magical dust pixies exuded, if prepared correctly, worked like a hallucinogen. Pixies themselves even started selling their dust when they wanted to make a quick buck, and some of them ran their own businesses with it.

"Imagine that. This proposed deed *involves* a pixie," I spat, ignoring the patron attention we'd managed to grab as well as Tambie, who stood idly by but poised to take action if necessary.

The shadows grew denser around Erebus' shoulders and head,

his eyes filling with liquid darkness until the whites disappeared. "If you're going to accuse me of something, wine god, why don't you fucking say it?"

My beast remained on edge, and despite my claws making my hands ache in anticipation, I held back. Instead, I produced my thyrsus and pointed the threatening end at the primordial's face. "A pixie was found murdered last night. And what is the easiest way to secure dust when one isn't a willing participant?" My gaze grew into a deep amber, fierce and glowing with ferocity.

Erebus pressed his palms against the table. With deliberate slowness, he rose, his form floating from the shadows' assistance. "I do not need to steal the dust, Dionysus. What I offer the pixies in exchange can't be matched. They've practically lined up at my door."

My grip tightened on the staff, my skin squeaking against the Olympus forged metal. "You didn't deny it."

"Um, boss?" Tambie's sweet, mouse-like voice chimed in. "Do you need me to ask you two to step outside, or did you intend to do that yourself?"

My gaze never faltered from Erebus as we stared each other down. Erebus's darkness curled over him like inky wings, slithering toward me. Conjuring my magic, I countered it with tendrils of maroon mist, forming an invisible shield.

"Pixies aren't a threat to me. Despite what you might think, I don't kill for sport," Erebus spat, his nails digging into the table as he combated my magic with his.

Unfortunately, he wasn't entirely lying. Had he killed and maimed in battle? In the very early ages, more times than I could count. Had he cheated, stolen, and deceived? Also, more times than I could count, but none of *that* pointed to murder.

Snarling, I lowered my staff. "I really fucking hate you, you know that?"

A satisfied smirk slid over Erebus's lips, a fake pout following. "Aw, did I spoil your triumphant moment of grandeur, Dion? Storming in here to solve the case and save the day before anyone else?" Erebus pushed past my magic enough to make his shadows tug my beard before recoiling.

I lifted my hand in a choking gesture only to have Tambie swoop in front of me, batting my arm away. She stood between me and Erebus, turning toward him first. "You—behave. And you—" She turned back to me, poking me in the chest. "Boss, I need help lifting some kegs behind the bar."

"Get Daevas to do it. He's working tonight," I countered, spinning the staff in my grip and glaring daggers at Erebus.

"No, he switched nights with Lillith to have a beach date with that sea nymph. Did you forget? You even signed off on it." Tambie waved her hands in front of my face, gaining my attention.

"Right. Yeah. I've had a lot going on," I grumbled, pointing my thyrsus at the primordial as we moved toward the bar. "I'm watching you."

Erebus's crew rejoined him in the booth, and he lit another cigar. "I'll be sure to be entertaining."

"A lot going on, such as a mating bond with a gorgeous red-haired lady witch?" Tambie grinned and hopped on her heels, moving behind the bar.

Squinting at her and her profound damnable intuition, I grabbed a keg with one hand and placed it in the kegerator with ease. "How the Tartarus did you know we accepted it?"

Tambie clapped her hands and squealed—a high-pitched bout of shrieking to rival a siren or fuck, to rival a *banshee*. "I just assumed, but I know now."

"Fuck," I grumbled, grabbing the other keg and hoisting it in. "We accepted it, yeah, but—"

Tambie gasped and felt around my body, pulling my shirt up and exposing my back. "You haven't *claimed*."

Snarling, I batted her hands away and yanked my shirt down. "No, I haven't, and I can't be sure she even wants that, but *why* are you checking *me* for a mark?"

"Isn't that how it works? She'd bite you, too?" Tambie fiddled with one of her antlers, tilting her head to the side.

Shaking my head, I connected the tubing for the carbon oxide tank. "She's a witch. She doesn't bite *me*. Shit, I don't even know if witches can claim in the same way." I was stammering, and I knew it, feeling like a tool.

"I don't know, that sounds positively delicious to me," a female voice said, her tone all too alluring for my comfort.

Vila, the succubus. Fuck me sideways.

"This conversation doesn't concern you, Vila," I clipped, throwing the door to the kegerator down and locking it.

Vila frowned and leaned her forearms on the bar top, purposely squishing her tits together beneath her low-cut, skintight black dress. "It's such a pity Chelsea would want nothing to do with it. Why would she have ever accepted a mating bond with a *beast* in the first place?"

Turning toward her, ignoring Tambie's pleas of protest, I caged Vila in with my arms, glowering down at her and huffing out of my nose. "What did I just say?"

Disregarding any imposing nature, Vila reached for my horn and stroked it just as I felt a familiar presence from—my *mate*.

Twenty-Seven

Chelsea

Following behind two witches leading me to a cottage nestled in a wood thicket hadn't been on my to-do list today, yet here I was. They didn't give off threatening vibes that I could tell, but considering a pixie was dead and one they had a connection with to boot, I remained cautious. We hadn't spoken at all during the walk, which in itself already put me on edge. I've always been a talker and built a career around it. Nonetheless, I respected their wishes for silence and used the time to keep vigilant of my surroundings.

An empty pit had formed in my stomach from Dion's absence. I had no basis for comparison, considering I'd never accepted a mating bond before now, but nothing could've prepared me for the physical ache from us being apart. Perhaps it would improve with time? Or the more harrowing alternative—it could get worse. Pressing my hands to my belly, I summoned my magic, attempting to lessen the hollow feeling, but I failed.

"It's new," the taller witch said, pausing long enough to give me a weak, reassuring smile. "It's going to feel like a part of your soul is missing for a while until the bond can settle."

I gulped and curled some of my rogue hair behind my ear. "Do you have a mate?"

"Yes," she replied, walking again, the cottage within arm's reach now. "A demon. He works in Bacchus on the weekends."

"What a small world, huh?" A meager, nervous laugh pushed from my throat as I stood on the threshold to the cottage, the witches waiting for me inside.

The shorter witch lowered her hood, a pair of chocolate-colored eyes peering at me. "You'll come to find it's not so small after all."

Gulping, nerves pricking my skin, I took one step, and an invisible weight pushed on my head and shoulders, making me stagger backward. It was enough to make me grab the doorway. Otherwise, I'd have fallen onto my ass. "Is this a trick or something?"

The two witches exchanged bewildered glances. "You can't get past the ward?"

Grimacing, I slid another foot forward, that same pressure intensifying. "Apparently not. I feel like a giant thumb is crushing me."

"You *are* new." The shorter one folded her arms. "Use your magic. Show the shield who you are. Tell it *what* you are, and the pressure will lift."

Grunting from the strain, I widened my stance and held up my palms, calling to my magic. My eyes pinched shut, and piece by piece, I began to relax, starting at my feet and working to my head. My power misted from my skin with little effort, curling in the air around me, lashing the ward, and then caressing it. After several more seconds of the shield deciphering the power I possessed, it finally lifted, and I opened my eyes.

"Very good," the taller witch said, smiling. "You're a quick study."

"Or just stubborn and prone to hyper-focusing," I countered, smirking.

The two witches parted and invited me inside with beckoning arms. There was a towering unlit hearth at the back of the space, wooden, dusty floorboards, a chandelier with black candles, and a simple table with three chairs. As I moved closer, the pentagram drawn on the floor with salt came into view, and I had to stifle a gasp. It had already begun to feel real, but seeing this, being in this space with two other witches, it started to resemble a fever dream.

"Is this where you practice and conjure spells?" I crouched near the pentagram.

"What? This place doesn't look homey enough to qualify as an abode?" The shorter witch asked, amusement bouncing in her tone.

I shot up, my hands erratically waving in front of me. "I meant absolutely no disrespect. I assumed from the lack of beds and—"

They both laughed, the taller one wiping a tear from her eye.

"Thank you, Chelsea," the taller one said, still chuckling. "We needed a good laugh."

Not knowing what to do with my hands, I folded them behind my back. "You're welcome. I think?"

The shorter one stepped forward with an outstretched hand and a warm smile. "My name is Amara, and this is my sister, Brigid."

After shaking both their hands and feeling each of their magic wrap around me in a comforting embrace, I knew this was a safe space. The tension melted away, replaced by curiosity, wonder, and a sudden eagerness to learn.

"Come, sit," Brigid encouraged, pulling out a chair. "I'm sure you have a lot of questions, and we have a few for you as well.

Amara, would you mind?" She pointed at the ceiling.

Amara flickered her fingers, vibrant tendrils of orange spiraling toward the chandelier and lighting the candles. Once satisfied, she sat at the table.

"I do have a lot of questions, but I'm honestly not sure where to start," I answered, resting my hands on the table to keep from fidgeting.

"Let us start with one, then, to pave the way." Amara scanned my hair. "How long have you known you're a witch?"

Fear wrenched my spine because I wasn't sure I wanted to admit it. I dropped my gaze to my palms, and my knee bounced beneath the table, making it vibrate.

Brigid's attention darted straight to it, and she tilted her head. "You have no reason to fear us, Chelsea. There are no right or wrong answers here. We're merely curious about the extent of your magic."

"The truth is—" I found the courage to look them in the eye. "I've only known for several days. I moved to Arcane Cove *before* I knew I had magic. I had no idea this place was magical, but something lured me here."

"Your mate, perhaps?" Amara suggested, glancing at her sister, who nodded. "And maybe even us as well."

The questions became clearer now, and I scooted forward on my seat. "The High Priestess told me I was a moon witch. Are all witches categorized like this?"

The sisters grinned at each other, this news exciting them.

"A moon witch. We couldn't have asked for anything more fitting. But yes, to answer your question. I'm a green witch, while Amara here—" Brigid rested a hand on her sister's shoulder. "—is a sun witch."

My chest tightened, and I gripped my mother's pentagram charm.

"My mother, she, too, was a sun witch." I slouched, sadness seeping its way in.

"Was?" Amara asked, frowning and reaching a hand across the table to rest on top of mine. "When did you lose her?"

I didn't pull away from Amara's touch but welcomed it. While it wasn't grounding like Dion's, it still gave a different kind of comfort, one that my sister Elani could always provide. "I was a small child, and I never knew she was a witch."

"Fate is such a mysterious vixen, isn't she?" Brigid rested her chin on her hand. "Would you care to try a spell with us? I have no doubt our connection of three will be strong, but it never hurts to test it."

Those nerves were at it again, and this time, they made my throat dry. "Could you tell me her name first?"

They both arched their brows.

"The sister you lost. If I'm to replace her potentially, I think it only respectful to know that much about her."

Amara sniffled as if holding back tears, and through a cracked voice, she answered, "Sage. She'd been our third for nearly a century."

A century? I didn't want to be rude and focus on that particular piece of information, but the ages of these women quickly elicited a raging curiosity.

"Again, I'm terribly sorry for your loss."

Brigid stared at the table with a fixed gaze, like she was recalling a memory. "She was a very talented forest witch and a bright light in the darkness."

"But now—" Amara started, garnering my attention before

continuing. "—you bring the moon's glowing brightness to us."

It all felt so right. Arriving in Arcane Cove. Dion became my mate. My destiny as a witch. Now, finding a sisterhood.

"I haven't performed any spells yet. Can you teach me?" I extended both hands for them to take.

With emphatic grins, they squeezed my hands and stood, guiding me to the pentagram. They ushered me to the highest point while they took positions at the lower two. They kept hold of my hands, and the magic surging through us was almost overwhelming. Subdued fury suddenly came out of nowhere. I ground my teeth and staggered backward, their grips tightening on me.

"Chelsea? Are you alright?" Brigid asked, a concerned trembling in her voice.

Fury. Concern. Anger. Calm.

It was all over the place, and I shook my head. Dion. His intense emotions were traveling through our bond. How was that possible?

"It's my mate. I don't know what's going on, but he seems to be on the verge of exploding. I—" I opened my eyes to find them staring at me.

"Go to him," Amara encouraged, letting go of my hand. "Spells can wait."

When Brigid let go, the magic receded, and I panicked. "What about the coven? Do I still have an opportunity to join you?"

The sisters shared a silent moment before Brigid squeezed my shoulders. "We would love to have you as our third, Chelsea if you wish to have us as your sisters."

"I'd be honored," I whispered, tears stinging my sinuses. "Thank you. I'll reach out when I can."

"You might consider claiming your mate soon, by the way," Brigid answered.

I'd turned for the door but slowly spun on my heel. "Claiming?"

"Yes. It helps to make the emotional tether less intense."

My power hummed at the prospect.

"I have no idea how to do that."

Brigid gave a charming grin. "You will when the time is right."

Nodding, I turned away, but a morbid curiosity gnawed at my insides. "One more thing—" Hesitation silenced me before I swallowed it down. "—Dionysus, he's immortal—"

"Chelsea," Brigid started, a gentle smile gracing her lips. "Witches take on the lifespans of those they are mated with, whether it be human or mythical god."

I returned Brigid's smile. I would've taken any years the universe saw fit to grant us, but this knowledge unleashed a newfound brightness in my heart.

After giving them one final glance, my newly appointed witch sisters, I left the cottage and made my way to Bacchus.

The pulsing bass echoed outside of the club building, and a disturbing sense settled into my bones. Something wasn't right. The urge to protect what was mine tugged at my spine and had me storming into the club, the bouncer shutting up once he recognized who I was—the club owner's *mate*. I clamored inside, my nose poised, and I picked up his scent instantaneously. He stood behind the bar, and a woman draped over it, stroking his horn. *My* fucking horn. The moon lent me its glow, making my skin iridescent and displaying my power.

Dion shrugged away from her touch, irritation pulsing through him in waves, and he lifted a finger in the woman's face. He was fuming now, yelling at her, telling her to go away, but she wasn't having it. I pushed through the crowds; my gaze narrowed on the greedy bitch going after what she knew was mine. And that only made it worse.

"Hey," I shouted, slipping my hands to my hips and waiting for her to turn around.

Dion's heated gaze panned over me, his eyes roaming the lunar glow and the "I'm not in the mood for this shit" expression I displayed.

The woman finally gave me the courtesy of meeting me face to face, and she flashed one of the most flippant, nonchalant smirks she could muster. She leaned her elbows on the bar top and parted her lips to speak.

Before she could get a single syllable off her tongue, I flicked my hand at her, gluing her mouth and making it impossible for her to speak.

Terror flooded her eyes, and she frantically grabbed at her mouth, mumbling and trying to talk. Dion gripped the metal table behind him, denting it and staring at me with a ferocity that had me aching in my core for him.

Snatching the woman's face, I used my magic to keep her still, to *listen* to me. "I sure hope you know how to eat through your asshole because I won't lift this spell until you apologize to anyone you've bespelled, to Dion, to me, and any other unbeknownst being you've manipulated."

She squirmed against my touch, her shoulders shrugging, and more mumbling followed.

"How do you apologize when you can't speak, you might ask?" I brought her face closer to mine. "Write it, type it, spell it out with fucking Cheerios for all I care, but I won't budge until you've turned a new leaf. Do you understand me?"

She emphatically nodded and rushed past me, hiding her face from customers who stared at her. My magic swelled in my chest, the white tendrils spiraling around me as if in approval of what I'd just done.

Dion, too, showed appreciation in the heat that still danced in his gaze like an unruly flame. He leaped over the bar, moving in front of me, his hands finding my hips. "That was—" Pausing, he massaged my waist and pulled me closer. "Chelsea, let me claim you." His nose grazed my neck, his canines scraping against the skin there. "No one would dare try something like that again when they could smell your power on me."

Claim him. You'll know what to do when the time comes.

Nuzzling Dion's neck with my forehead, I moved my lips to his ear, gently nipping the lobe. "Take us to your sanctuary, Dion," I whispered, digging my nails into the taut muscle in his arms.

A bubbling growl vibrated in his chest, deeper than I'd ever heard it. The sound, with all its underlying meaning and promise, had my heart racing. Dion didn't bother walking us to the VIP door. He wrapped me in his burly embrace and ported us straight there, waving his hand behind him to make daylight disappear. The sky melted into black velvet sprinkled with glowing white dust, and a full moon appeared—bright and resplendent. The illumination charged my power, the magic striking every neuron before it floated from my skin.

We'd accepted our mating bond. Now it was time to claim each other's *beasts*.

Twenty-Eight

Chelsea

Dion's horns grew more pronounced, his jawline more angular, his claws thicker, and the amber in his eyes became reflective from the moon's glow. I smiled at how handsome he always has been, but *this* form stood out as him at his most primal. Stepping toward him, I used my magic to dematerialize my clothes, flittering them away as stardust.

I pressed a hand to Dion's cheek, grinning resplendently at him, his chest heaving as if he was holding back something. "My mate," I cooed, emphasizing the word I knew his beast yearned to hear repeated over and over for eternity.

That otherworldly growl vibrated in his throat again, and Dion pressed his forehead to mine. "Chelsea, I don't want to hurt you."

The words came out pinched as if he was vulnerable to admitting it. I raised on the balls of my feet and traced my finger over the same horn that damn succubus had the nerve to touch, wiping all essence of her away so there was only my scent left on him. "You won't," I whispered. "Your beast wants to claim me, Dion. To fuck me. Hurting and killing are reserved for those who do us *wrong*."

Crimson flashed in Dion's gaze before he pointed behind me. "Then *run*."

Blinking because his reply took me by absolute surprise, I backpedaled with an uneasy hand pressed to my chest. "What?" I breathed out.

The claws on Dion's feet scraped the ground. "I am to chase you to claim you. So, run, *mágissa*."

My magic pooled in my core, tightening there in understanding. We were to play the fox and hound. Once he caught me—a wicked grin played on my lips, and I turned, sprinting through the forest with my bare breasts welcoming the moonlight.

There would've been no way of telling Dion was hot on my heels straight away, but the leaves crunching from first my left side, then the right, were a dead giveaway. If this were any other situation, I might have worried about my glowing skin giving my position away, but with my mate, I wanted it to be easy to find me—I wanted him to *claim* me.

"Chelsea," Dion growled before whisking into the shadows undetectable. He was toying with me, and by the moon and stars, I *loved* it.

My breathing grew more erratic the more I ran, my heart racing from the excitement and effort. A chill formed through the trees, making my breath smokey and the moonbeams peeking through the branches foggy. I slowed my steps, no longer hearing Dion anywhere around me. Snarling, Dion pounced from the shadows, toppling both of us to the soft, mossy ground. He'd cradled my head and pressed some of his weight at my back, pinning me beneath him.

"Caught you," Dion whispered, smiling against my shoulder and peppering my skin with light kisses.

His already hardened length grazed my ass, and I dug my nails into the dirt, tearing away bits of grass. How would it feel? How would this time be different from the others?

I raised my ass as much as I could with him on top of me. "I'm yours for the taking, Dionysus."

Dion's beast let out a gravelly hum, and he traced his canines delicately down my back, lightly nipping one of my ass cheeks. He curled a finger over my entrance, checking how moist I was. I was *drenched*. A satisfied snarl echoed through the surrounding trees, and he pressed the tip of his cock at my entrance, pushing in slowly at first until he thrust it the rest of the way. I cried out, the connection we now had heightening the sensations.

Dion pressed a hand between my shoulder blades, lowering my head to the moss and pinning me. His thrusts were ferocious and wild with guttural grunts. My toes curled against the emerald moss beneath us, and fluttering orgasms washed over me in repeated waves that had me in a euphoric daze. It kept taking me to the point where I didn't think I could stand it any longer; the sensations were just so incredibly delicious, and then it'd taper away only to drive right back to my core.

Dion's hands moved to my waist, hoisting me to my hands and knees. His pumping slowed, but he bent forward, kissing my nape, licking it. He tested me at first, scraping his teeth in the spot he intended to leave his mark. When I reached for him, tangling my fingers in his wavy, dark locks, he sank his canines into my neck. I wailed, but not from pain. It pinched at first, a sting as his teeth punctured, but it was instantly replaced by a pleasuring, calming swirl that traveled from where he claimed me through my chest and stomach, and tightened in my clit.

Blood trickled over my collarbone and in between my breasts. The euphoria built to a crescendo of pulsating pleasure bursting through every neuron of my fucking existence. My magic beamed from my skin, curling around us, fusing us, and I could have sworn the moon shone even brighter because of it. When Dion released me from his beast's hold, the teeth letting go of my neck, he lapped the wound, sealing it from bleeding but leaving behind a claiming scar I'd be proud to bear.

Dion's thrusts picked up again, and I reached for him, latching onto his forearm. "Wait."

Pausing with his hands on my hips, the beast let out a disapproving growl, but Dion arched a brow at me, doing as I asked. Turning around, I lay on my back, spreading my knees wide and encouraging him to cage me in. Grinning, he fell over top of me, propping his elbows on each side of my head, and began his frenzied thrusts, ready to undo himself inside me, *craving* it. Charging myself with the moon's lunar graces, I slid my hands to his back and dug my nails into his skin enough to leave marks and dragged them downward.

Dion tilted his head back, roaring at what I was doing, but it didn't stop me. I claimed my mate in my own way, creating tattooed markings of the lunar cycle up his spine. At the top point where his neck met his head, I carved a prominent crescent moon—the same phase of the night when we first met. With the moonlight serving as ethereal ink, my claiming mark would glow on him whenever I was near. Finishing, I bucked my hips, meeting him thrust for thrust now, encouraging him.

After several more feral thrusts, our skin slapping against each other, he came undone inside of me, tensing and shaking. His hips jerked until he relaxed, flopping over me and brushing my sweat-soaked hair from my forehead. "I didn't know witches could do that."

"Neither did I," I mused, trailing my toes over his thigh. "My sisters told me."

"Well—" Dion started, peering over his shoulder at my glowing claiming mark. "—I fucking dig it."

Smiling up at him and the view of the moon giving him a shimmering white outline, I curled a finger around one horn and pulled him closer, kissing him. "What's next for us, Dion?"

"Does there have to be a next?" Dion tilted his head, lazily dragging a finger over where he'd bit me.

The thought of the unknown, the bright future as I learned more of my magic, conjuring spells with my new coven and exploring the Cove with my *mate*, had my body going boneless. "No, I suppose there doesn't *have* to be a next."

"Exactly," Dion gruffly whispered, settling between my thighs again. "And this is coming from the god of 'living it up,' but one of the best parts of living, Red, is *living* for the present moments."

"You honestly still think that after how long you've been around?"

Dion used his thumb to scratch under his bottom lip. "Nah. I've lived over a thousand years, Chelsea, but my life didn't truly start—" Dion pressed a chaste kiss to my lips. "—until I found my mate."

My moon magic buzzed, and as I stared into his eyes, knowing he'd never lie or fabricate anything with me, I crashed my mouth against his.

"Can I ask you something, D?" I kept my arms wrapped around his strong neck.

"Anything."

Tracing my fingertip over the curve of one horn, I asked, "None of the other gods have a beast form like this. Is there a particular reason that *you* do?"

Dion smiled, flashing a bit of canine. "It was the second or maybe third time, I can't remember, that Hera tried to kill me. Despite them making an arrangement to be married for politics only and that they were free to be with other people, she was still furious that I was the first product of Zeus's *grazing*." Dion paused, scratching his thumb under his bottom lip. "When she almost succeeded the time before, Zeus wanted to protect me. The only way he could do that—was by cursing me with the beast."

"It's by no means a curse," I reassured him.

He bumped a knuckle under my chin. "It used to be when I couldn't control it as well as I do now."

"It *saved* you. Maybe that's why it took so long for us to find each other." Grinning, I pressed a light kiss to his lips.

"I'd have learned to control it in an instant if I knew it would bring you to me that much sooner, Chels." Dion trailed his claws through my hair with a contented sigh.

One hundred and four starbursts shot through the sky that night—one for each day I'd wasted knowing Dion and being too scared and stubborn to be with him. With him, I'd found a new home in Arcane Cove. I discovered my true self and uncovered a deeper connection with my late mother that I had never known I had. And though I never admitted my jealousy over my little sister's mythical life—here I was, a part of the magic all along.

Epilogue

Dion

Three months later…

"Thanks, man, you can set those over there," I said to the delivery man proudly displaying the UMPS logo on his navy blue shirt—the United Magical Package Service delivering more ambrosia wine from Olympus.

Bacchus numbers had sky-rocketed since Chelsea and I became mates. I'd like to have thought it was the extra pulse of magical energy floating through the Cove from our bond, but I knew the biggest reason currently stood on stage with his annoyingly brightened white smile.

Apollo became a headliner every Saturday fucking night, and everyone came in droves to sing along with his songs, rock out, and throw articles of clothing at him. Chelsea had also worked her PR magic without any aid from me or her witchcraft, securing an additional three acts—a dancing violinist, aerial dancers, and a magic act. That's right. A mythie performing human sleight of hand tricks as a spectacle *here*. My mate was a godsdamned genius.

Tambie tapped my elbow and pointed at the bar. Herb gruffly sat on a stool hunched over a tumbler of whiskey, and the sight made me blanch. Bacchus had never been Herb's scene. In fact, I couldn't recall a time *ever* seeing him here. He'd always been more of a Finneas' Pub type.

"I'll see what's going on," I said to Tambie, patting her shoulder.

Tambie frowned and scraped a nail over one of her antlers. "I sure hope it's not another murder. I *still* think about that poor pixie, and I didn't even know her."

Chelsea and I had offered our help countless times in investigating who killed the witch pixie, especially since she'd been a former sister in Chelsea's new coven. The sheriff, as stubborn and crotchety as ever, told us all forms of "go to hell" and to let him do his damn job. Three months later, the trail toward her killer only went colder.

Moving behind the bar, I leaned on one palm and pointed at the sheriff's empty glass. "Can I freshen you up there, Herb?"

"Damn straight you can and make it something stronger, would ya?" Herb slid the glass closer.

Grabbing a fresh bottle of ambrosia wine, I swirled my magic around it, altering its contents to taste like bourbon while maintaining the wine's potency, and poured him a double. "Considering I've never seen you in here, you'll understand why I'm curious as to your patronage tonight?"

Herb let out a gruff sigh and snatched the newly filled glass, immediately shoving his nose into it to guzzle. "You're right. This place is obnoxious, loud as all get out, and everyone shows far too much skin for my taste."

Chuckling, I propped an elbow on the bar. "Gee, Herb. Tell me how you really feel about *my* establishment."

"Sorry, Dion. The truth is, this was the only place I hadn't thought to look for a suspect." Herb paused to lick whiskey droplets that collected on his thick mustache. "I just can't wrap my head around it. Whoever it was, murdered that poor female in cold blood, left zero evidence, and then seemingly disappeared."

"You make it sound like they had plans to do it again. Maybe this was something personal, and they skipped town?" I scanned the club for anyone who might be nervously watching us.

Herb scratched his scalp. "That's the thing. This pixie wouldn't have harmed a fly, went out of her way to help people, and from how most folks described her, she had the type of personality that lit up a damned room."

Nodding, I tapped my finger on the bar top. "You know what I want to say to all of this, right?"

The sheriff swiped the tumbler into his grasp, lifting it and pointing at me. "I'll ask for help when I'm good and ready for it, boy. In the meantime, I'm going to *mingle*."

He'd said the word mingle as if it was difficult to push from his throat before sliding off the stool. Hermes and Bruce were quick to scoop him up, waving me off like taking the crotchety porcupine under their wings was no big deal.

Smiling and shaking my head, I made eye contact with Tambie and gave her a thumbs up to indicate there wasn't additional bad news. A tingle zipped down my spine, an invisible tether tugging at my bond with Chelsea. She needed me. A devilish grin played on my lips, and I ported straight to my apartment, which was now *ours*.

Chelsea stood at the window with one hand raised skyward, her moonlight glow damn near lustrous from the full moon tonight. She'd had her back to me but slowly turned when she sensed my presence. The expression she gave me wasn't what I had expected. She looked—*surprised?*

"Chels? Did you not call on me?" I raised a brow, my nose picking up several other female scents overlapping each other.

"Babe, I didn't think it'd work that quickly," Chelsea admitted, a light burp following.

Scanning the surroundings, I noted several empty bottles of ambrosia wine and Riley chasing a grey *cat*. A mouse squeaked, zooming toward my feet, and I lifted a boot so the tiny creature didn't run into me. "Oh, light of my life. What the Tartarus is going on?"

"Sorry," Amara's voice chirped. She scurried from the hallway, chasing after the mouse, scooping it into her palms once she caught it.

Elani, Chelsea's sister, emerged next from the hallway, holding my saved rum bottle from the eighteenth century when I'd had a very brief career on a pirate crew. "I looked all over, Chels, but this was all I could—" Elani froze when she spotted me, and her pale pink wings drooped.

"Dion," Chelsea started, clutching something in her fist and slipping an arm around my waist. "This was a surprise I didn't know was happening. They all showed up unannounced, and I couldn't rightly turn them away."

"Hey, Dion," Elani added, smiling brightly, bits of her copper appearing in her dark brown hair when the ceiling lights hit it at the right angles. "Long time, no see."

With Chelsea draped over my shoulders, I extended a hand for the prized bottle Elani held. "Nice to see you too, sis. But what is this surprise? It isn't her birthday."

Amara moved closer, stroking her mouse familiar with a single finger. "We thought we'd throw you both a mated party, but Elani couldn't make it out to the Cove until recently."

"We were getting ready to bless your bond with favor when Bacchus closed so you could be here too," Brigid answered, appearing with several items cradled in her arms and a wooden bowl. A bat perched on her shoulder, its veiny black wings folded back.

Chelsea kissed my cheek and opened her hand, revealing the small white crystal resting on her palm. "I was letting the moon charge it."

"Well then, do your thing, ladies. Don't let me get in the way." Pinching Chelsea's chin between two fingers, I pulled her lips to mine, kissing her. "And next time you need more booze for *any* occasion, just ask me, sweetheart." I arched a brow at Elani, who averted her gaze, whistling and pretending she had no idea I referenced the rum bottle she'd pilfered from my stash.

Moving to the kitchen, I set the bottles upright, sending spirals of burgundy magic around them, filling each to the brim and, not bothering to cork them. Chelsea's emerald eyes locked onto me as she formed a triangle with her coven sisters, Elani joining me in the kitchen to watch from afar. Tears filled Elani's eyes as she peered at her big sister in her magical element, reciting spells, her glowing white magic entangling with the other witches' yellow and green magic.

"I know it's too late to reverse any of it, Lani, but are you okay with this?" I asked, filling my wine glass.

Elani looked at me perplexed. "Okay with what? You being my sister's fated mate?"

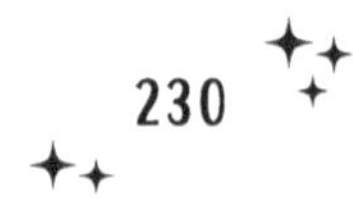

"Yeah," I whispered, uncomfortably rubbing the back of my neck.

Elani laughed and patted my arm, snatching one of the bottles and not bothering with a glass, drank from it. "Dion, I've been rooting for you both to get your heads out of your asses since the day Chelsea started texting me about how much she couldn't stand you when you all first met but also how much she could *not* stop thinking about you."

"You knew from the start, didn't you?" I asked, smiling.

"I'm a love-goddess. Of course, I knew. But I'm duty-bound to let you figure it out for yourself." Elani winked and raised the bottle to cheers.

The witches finished their spellbinding, Chelsea trotting to us with Riley curled around her neck. "What are you two talking about?"

Elani hugged her sister. "How much partying we plan to do tonight in your honor."

"Those are mighty bold words to say to the frenzy god, sis," Chelsea replied, laughing nervously and giving me a concerned look over Elani's shoulder.

Still grinning like a damned lovesick fool, I held a palm out to her, reassuring her that I'll make sure Elani was able to get home to her love-god husband and kid.

When they requested a party in my and my mate's honor, I couldn't help but pull out all the stops. Music blasted late into the night; the sound drowned from nearby neighbors with my magic. There was dancing, singing, and a crazy game of Pictionary that I purposely made every drawing of mine look like a dick. With the moon favoring my beautiful witch, it honored us with a cloudless sky for the duration of the night, ensuring its glow never faltered.

And by Olympus, the *drinking*. At one point, I started pouring Elani's drinks with zero alcohol, and she still whooped and hollered like nothing had changed. Brigid and Amara pulled Elani to the side, enlightening her about all things witchy and how female bloodlines pass down the magic through their daughters.

I took the opportunity to yank my mate into the hallway, pinning her against the wall and pressing a hand above her head. "Hey," I teased.

"Hey, you," Chelsea answered, fiddling her fingers over the top of my pants. She grinned at something behind me.

It was nearly pitch black in the hallway, but her claiming tattooed mark glowed from underneath my white T-shirt, illuminating it as if it were daylight.

Letting out a satisfied growling purr, I turned back to Chelsea, kissing her. "Glowing bright to let all others know I'm *yours*." I trailed my lips to my bite scar displayed proudly above her collarbone and kissed her there. The scar had gotten lighter since I'd first given it to her and became a piece of art that formed a perfect circle.

"I see a lot of low-cut tops in my future," Chelsea mused, her petite fingers touching my abs through my shirt. "Because I'm *obsessed* with how I feel showing everyone who my mate is."

Sliding my tongue over my mark gracing her skin, I let out an appreciating snarl. "All thanks to the Cove, Red."

The doorbell rang, followed by several loud thuds from someone knocking. My body instinctually went into protective mode, and I tensed. "Were you all expecting anyone else?"

"No. Not that I'm aware of," Chelsea answered, the skin on her

forehead cinching in concern.

"I'll get it," I yelled to the drunken witches and goddess in the living room. Storming for the door with Chelsea following, I pressed my eye to the peephole.

A laugh poured out of me at the sight of Harmony Makos standing with a hand on her hip, annoyance plain in her expression. She rolled her eyes and knocked again.

"Dion, who is it?" Chelsea asked.

Still chuckling, I whipped open the door. "Hey, Harm."

"*Hey?*" Harm's gaze flicked between my face and the mark on Chelsea's neck. "That's all you have to say to me, Dino, is *hey?*"

It'd been too long since I heard the nickname Dino, given to me by Harm herself, when she'd repeatedly gotten my name wrong and never bothered to correct herself. The smile had yet to fall from my lips.

"Harm?" Chelsea squeaked, moving past me to tackle her best friend in the hallway.

Harm hugged Chelsea but pushed her back by her shoulders, holding her captive. "Chels, I go off on godly war duties for a few months, and I come back to forty-two texts and an invitation to a mated party? Mated. To Dionysus, might I add? And you're a *witch?*" Harm spoke erratically, but the happiness radiating in her eyes was more than obvious.

"We've got so, so much to talk about, friend," Chelsea answered, tears filling her eyes as she pulled Harm in for another hug.

Elani moved beside me with her arms folded before proceeding to brush imaginary dust from her shoulders.

"This your doing?" I asked, soaking in the sight of my mate happy and content.

"Yup. Eros put me up to it. Something about taking a photo of your face when you realized Harm knows you are ferally mated to her best friend now," Elani added.

"Harm? Harm would never—" I paused when Harmony tossed me a seething glare, pointing at me.

"Dino, we *also* need to talk."

"Oh, shit." My face fell blank, and Elani lifted her phone, a camera shutter sound going off.

"That's the one," Elani beamed.

Aside from a punch in the shoulder and a long-winded speech on how she'd figure out a way to end my immortal life if I hurt Chelsea, Harmony spent most of her time catching up with us and joining in on the festivities. We partied until the sun rose, leaving my mate especially tired once the moon's power wasn't as strong. Chelsea fell asleep with her head resting in my lap while Elani took one of my shoulders and Harm the other. If you'd told me a year ago three beautiful women would surround me and I had plans to do unspeakable acts in the bedroom with only *one* of them later, I'd have laughed into oblivion.

Now, with the women I called family through fate's design that brought us all together, I nestled into the couch, my protective nature satiated with them in my arms. And the beast, for the first time in eons, could finally feel *peace*.

STAY TUNED FOR BOOK 2 IN

THE
Mythical Mates
OF
Arcane Cove

Scan the QR Code Below to Check Out More of my Works!

@authorcarlyspade on all social media

linktr.ee/authorcarlyspade

STAY TUNED!

WWW.CARLYSPADE.COM

Books by Carly Spade

Acknowledgments

Thank you to everyone who has supported me through this process of creating and starting a new series. Monster romance wasn't something I ever considered, but now am beyond excited to become a part of this niche and rub elbows with some of my favorite authors in the genre. Much like my Contemporary Mythos series, I didn't want to delve into this genre of romance until I had something new to bring to the table. Incorporating characters from mythology, folklore and fairytales within the cozy small town fantasy vibes seemed to be the right choice. ☺

Thank you, Cerys, for being my cheerleader as usual and already displaying such excitement for the next book which at the time of this I haven't written a word of yet. LOL. And AK, you're my absolute ROCK when it comes to writing and I'll always be so thankful for your support and friendship. And to my husband, your continued support with my book business as a whole just means the world to me and I can't tell you how much I appreciate you for it.

To my loyal readers, you'll find some familiar faces in this new series and a lot of fresh faces, but I hope you enjoy it just as much as my other worlds. ☺

To the new readers, welcome! Your support of indie authors is continually appreciated and I hope to help you escape life's troubles, put a smile on your face, and make you positively swoon. (Maybe fan yourself a bit too. ☺) Here's to new beginnings, horns, tails, and claws!

About the Author

CARLY SPADE is an adult romance writer who has been writing since she could pick up a pencil. After the insanity of obtaining a bachelor's and master's degree in cybersecurity, creating worlds to escape to still ate at her very soul. She started writing FanFiction (which can still be found if you scour the internet), and soon felt the need to get her original ideas on paper. And so the adventure began.

She lives in Colorado with her husband and two fur babies, and revels in an enemies to lovers trope with a slow burn.

Find her online:

WWW.CARLYSPADE.COM

www.ingramcontent.com/pod-product-compliance
Lightning Source LLC
Chambersburg PA
CBHW032248310726
48973CB00008B/2338